ff

THE BIRDS OF THE INNOCENT WOOD

Deirdre Madden

faber and faber
LONDON · BOSTON

First published in 1988
by Faber and Faber Limited
3 Queen Square London WC1N 3AU

Photoset by Parker Typesetting Service Leicester
Printed in Great Britain by
Mackays of Chatham Kent

British Library Cataloguing in Publication Data

Madden, Deirdre
The birds of the innocent wood
I. Title
823'.914[F] PR6063.A28/

ISBN 0-571-14880-8

THE BIRDS OF THE INNOCENT WOOD

by the same author

HIDDEN SYMPTOMS

For my sister, Angela Madden

CHAPTER ONE

The circumstances of Jane's early life were so tragic and romantic that at one time she drew solace from thinking that it might all be an elaborate fiction and that a happier truth would one day be revealed. She was an only child who had lived with her parents in a small house at the edge of the city, and at the age of two she fell ill: very seriously ill. It was even thought that she might die. And one night, when Jane was in hospital, her mother and father were both burnt to death in a fire which completely destroyed their family home. Shortly after that the little girl made an unexpected recovery from her illness, and on leaving hospital she went to live with her aunt, a tailoress who was much less upset by the death of her sister-in-law and her brother than she was by the necessity of taking her tiny orphaned niece under her comfortless wing.

The little girl's health remained poor, and for the next three years her life in her aunt's home was frequently interrupted by periods spent in hospital, a time she could later hardly remember. Of her aunt's house she retained a few vague, comforting images such as how she would sit in an upstairs alcove where the window was set with panes of coloured glass, and from there she could watch the common city sparrows become magical birds, stained red or green or blue as they hopped along the sill. She also remembered the white attic where she slept, and where she also spent most of her waking hours.

Much of the house frightened her. Most frightening of all was her aunt's workroom, with its vicious treadle sewing machine, the long, cruel-looking shears and, worst of all, the Judy: a huge headless, armless, legless thing of female shape, with long pins stuck into its stout baize breast. She thought of it as an independent creature and imagined that every night it moved malevolently up and down the workroom. Yet because of its daytime stillness and solidity she also saw it as a dead thing. She once tried to befriend it by thinking of it simply as 'Judy', but her aunt insisted upon the sinister prefix, and so the fear remained.

But what she remembered most significantly of her aunt's house were the long, long empty hours of silence. Her aunt was plainly not interested in her. She spoke to Jane only when it was absolutely necessary, otherwise she ignored her.

Hospital was not much worse than home. She remembered a clown who had come to the ward one day. He had made her laugh, but she was frightened of him too. She remembered excessive warmth, sweet drinks and fat black grapes, but above all she remembered being sick: remembered pain, vomiting, hallucinatory dreams and the horrifying sight of her own blood. Her treatment was almost as bad as the illness itself. Habitually they forced her to swallow medications which were bitter and dry in her mouth; they injected the base of her spine; they took blood samples from the crook of her arm; and when she was undressed and the doctors examined her, touching her body with brisk indifference, she would weep with loneliness and humiliation.

Sometimes when her pain was not too severe she would call out for her mother. She heard the other children do this. But when she suffered really intense physical pain, she forgot such niceties. Then she would simply scream and scream.

When Jane reached the age of five, her aunt used her ill health as an excuse to send the child away to a convent boarding school. She tried to engage Jane's sense of gratitude by telling her constantly of the great expense which this entailed. For a while Jane was indeed awed by the amount of money required for her fees, books and uniform; but this was sharply undercut when she saw the uniform itself. The gymslip was an ugly thing of heavy bottle-green worsted, and when she thought of the fine stuffs with which her aunt usually worked Jane thought that she had either been lying about the expense, or that she had been duped.

She would never forget the day on which she was first taken to the convent. Her aunt rang the bell, there was a shuffle of approaching feet; and then the heavy wooden door was swung open by a very small nun. She ushered them into the dim hallway, and they waited there for the Reverend Mother who, on her arrival, patted Jane on the head and then retired to a little parlour on the left of the hallway to speak with Jane's aunt.

The little nun (who told her that her name was Sister Imelda) then took Jane by the hand and led her down a long, bright corridor which ran at right angles to the hallway. As the child stepped into the corridor she gasped: she felt that she was in a tunnel filled with dazzling light, which destroyed time and space. There was height, coolness, paleness and the smell of flowers. When they came to the end of the corridor she wanted to say to the nun, 'That was like being nowhere.'

Sister Imelda had brought her to the chapel. Jane genuflected clumsily and knelt down at a pew of honey-coloured wood. She said a little prayer, then looked around her. The chapel was smaller, brighter and much, much cleaner than any of the city churches which she had attended with her aunt. The walls were pale blue, and on the east side tall french windows gave on to an orderly garden.

'Why is there a bird there?' she whispered loudly, pointing to a dove of white stone which was fixed above the altar.

'That's the Holy Ghost. He's the special patron of our congregation. We're the Little Sisters of the Paraclete.' Seeing the child open her mouth she anticipated the question and added quickly, 'Paraclete is another name for the Holy Ghost.'

The nun took Jane by the hand and led her out of the airy chapel, back down the beautiful corridor. This time she was not so dazzled that she was unable to appreciate the details. One entire side of the passage was glass from floor to ceiling and was hung with long white muslin curtains, some of which were buoyed up by waves of soft air from the open windows behind them. The grey marble floor was brilliantly polished; the wooden ceiling was high, curved and dark. Along the wall which faced the windows were religious statues of painted plaster which stood upon wooden plinths, and before each one there was a vase of flowers and a burning candle. The statues were interspersed with large paintings of religious subjects in ornate gilt frames; and the symmetry and the stillness of it all greatly pleased the child.

When they reached the parlour, they found that her aunt had already left.

Sister Imelda gave Jane some food to eat, and later took her upstairs to the dormitory. 'The other little girls will be here tomorrow,' she said, indicating five empty beds.

'Where are they now?' Jane asked as she sat down on the sixth bed.

'Now? Why, they're still at home with their mammys and daddys.'

'I haven't got a mammy or a daddy,' she said, and was surprised when Sister Imelda refuted this.

'Of course you have a mammy and a daddy. Everyone has parents.' And the nun then told her that all the other little girls would soon be obliged to leave their mammys and daddys. Jane's parents would still be with her, and were with her always, watching over her constantly, even while she slept. This was a new idea to Jane, and a very strange one. Sister Imelda added that anyone who believed in God need never be lonely. 'God is our Father in Heaven, and Mary is our divine Mother. And think too of all the host of saints and angels: they're our brothers and sisters. And aren't I your sister too? Don't you call me sister?'

Jane was not quite convinced by this line of reasoning, but she thought that it would be rude to say so. The following day, however, when the other little girls arrived with their parents, she was suddenly won round to Sister Imelda's way of seeing things. Jane hung back and covertly watched these real mothers, some of whom were plain, bossy lipsticked creatures in dowdy clothes; and these real fathers, some of whom looked shifty, stupid or cruel. Suddenly she was glad that she did not have such parents. She thought of her own mother who she now believed was also there. The scent of flowers in the pale corridor, that was her mother, and she was also the breeze that lifted the muslin curtains and the sunlight that streamed through the chapel's high windows, gilding the white stone dove.

Jane adapted easily to school life, for she was a docile and obedient child. The nuns noticed that she was extraordinarily self-contained, and that she made friends but not close friends. If anyone mistreated her, she simply ignored them. She also became extremely religious, and was often to be found wandering up and down the pale corridor, looking at the pictures and statues. One of the paintings showed St Francis of Assisi, diminutive and dark. He stood in his brown habit and sandals upon a hillside, arms upraised, and a long row of swallows swooped above his head in a delicate arc. Sister Imelda taught her the poem which he had written about Brother Sun and Sister Moon, and she used to think of it as she sat outside in the ordered garden. She told Sister Imelda that when she grew up she too wanted to be a nun.

The sisters first began to have trouble with Jane when she was nine years old, and developed the habit of taking the other little girls aside to tell them of her unfortunate infancy. She did this with a daemonic combination of eloquence and detachment, persisting with her story until her small listeners were crying and afraid. Eventually, Sister Imelda overheard her steady and calculated discourse and, although familiar with the child's background, the method of the telling chilled her. Jane was taken aside and sternly reprimanded; and when she persisted in behaving this way, more discreetly but also more often, she was severely punished. Yet still she would not stop. She loved manipulating the other little girls. Every time she told her story she felt as if she was leading the unsuspecting children to a vast black pit, and when she had taken them right to the edge, she would suddenly draw back and abandon them there. She craved their pity and their sense of horror; and at the same time she utterly despised the other little girls for allowing her to induce these feelings in them. It was her tragedy, and she was never so weak as to cry for the loss of her parents.

When she was twelve, she was confirmed. The nuns took

great pains to prepare the children for the sacrament, telling them of the first descent of the Holy Spirit, of the great wind which went through the house where the apostles waited; and of the tongues of fire which appeared above their heads. In the chapel, Jane looked at the stone dove and thought of how God's spirit would descend upon her. She thought that the other children did not realize the significance of this, but she knew that nothing could be more important.

She would never forget the ceremony. She waited in line, watching the bishop who was dressed in cloth of gold move slowly along the altar rails, confirming all the children. The bright church was filled with the sound of singing, and with the rich spicy smell of incense. And when the bishop came to her, time stopped. In the moment when he smeared chrism upon her forehead and touched her face gently with his fingers everything was contained: her mother and father's lives and deaths, her own past and all her unknown future, the love of her dead parents and the love of God: a feeling of simple peace and wholeness such as she had never known before. And in that moment her senses left her, so that she could no longer hear the choir or smell the incense or see the light. In that silent, scentless darkness she could only feel a hand upon her shoulder, and she did not believe that it was her sponsor. She believed that her dead mother stood behind her, and this consciousness of her mother's presence was overwhelming. It made death irrelevant, and when she returned blindly to her place in the body of the church, her heart was flooded with joy.

That joy carried her along for the rest of the day. They drank tea and ate buns in the school hall, and Sister Imelda was pleased to see how happy – ecstatic, even – Jane was, for she had feared that the loneliness of her orphaned state would have deeply affected her on that day. Later, however, when the nun noticed that the child had vanished, she felt uneasy. She sought Jane out in all the empty rooms of the school until at last she found her in the deserted chapel. Her joy was all gone. She was standing by a statue before which a row of little candles burned, and she looked white and shocked. Her right hand was wedged hard under her left arm, and she slowly rocked herself backwards and forwards. Through the french windows came voices and laughter as the other little girls and their parents took photographs in the garden.

'What is it, Jane? Tell me, dear, what happened.' But the child would not speak and when Sister Imelda tried to touch her, she jerked away.

She would not tell the nun that she had stolen happily away from the crowd to pray for her parents, but in lighting a candle for their dead souls she had accidentally burnt her fingers.

She changed after her confirmation. Now she found that when she was standing in front of the statue of Our Lady in the pale corridor she wanted more than the simple belief which she already had. She wanted Our Lady to step down warm with life from the wooden plinth; to feel herself being wrapped in her maternal embrace.

As she became older, she found it harder to maintain a steady belief in her parents and with adolescence came terrifying moments when her faith was shaken and she would suddenly think that there was no God. Our Lady and Christ himself had either never existed, or else they had all been something other than what people said they were. And there was no God because she had no parents. She, in herself, was a proof of the void, because of her motherless and fatherless state. It was so easy to believe in death and in emptiness, and so hard to believe in things for which she did not have physical proof, things which she had not seen.

It depressed her greatly that she had no memories of her parents. The fire in which they died had also destroyed all family photographs, and so she did not even know how her mother had looked. She would look at and touch her own body, telling herself that her mother had once existed in just such a form, but she could never really understand this. If only she could remember or imagine a swathe of scented hair, or a warm hand webbed with fine blue veins, then everything would have been so different.

She became conscious of the nuns as real women who had

renounced their homes, their families and the whole world to become brides of Christ. Habitually she would stare at the sisters when she thought that they were unconscious of her gaze, but she was always reprimanded: the nuns knew instinctively when they were being watched.

For years she accepted life in the convent because it was the only place where she had not been made to suffer, but this tolerance changed when one of the girls invited Jane home. She looked forward to this treat for days, but when it actually took place it shocked her. The child's family was almost aggressively happy. Large in number, they lived in a small house so that their bodies, their personalities and their lives seemed compressed and intensified; and the degree of intimacy which Jane felt was quite horrible. Washing dripped from a clothes horse on the kitchen ceiling, the hall was cluttered with tennis racquets, bikes, shoes, footballs and a huge kite. A radio roared in the living-room, and the rich greasy smell of fried food filled the air. The father of the house was sick in bed, but made his presence felt with frequent petitions for food and drink. Jane knew that he was up there with an absolute certainty which she could never feel about her own father. The child's mother was a cheerful slattern who, as the day progressed, filled an ashtray to overflowing with cigarette ends, stained with lipstick. Jane thought that she was wonderful, but later in the day when she absently ruffled Jane's hair and tried to hug her, the child instinctively shrank back.

When she went back to the convent that evening, she hated the stillness, the silence, the cleanliness and the order of the place; and that night in bed she cried as she had seldom cried before. She felt as if something had been violently ripped from her.

In the ensuing weeks Jane slowly withdrew her friendship from the other girl until she was completely frozen out, and there was no longer the danger of a second invitation. She never again agreed to visit any of her fellow pupils at home.

Gradually she had outgrown the habit of tormenting the other little girls with the story of her childhood, but the terrible craving which that habit had fed did not diminish. Instead, it grew to such a level that the mere pity of children whom she despised could do nothing to satisfy her. She therefore forced herself to cultivate an abnormally high level of self-control and detachment, and she brought to this all the strength and power of her will. The nuns watched uncomfortably as she slowly iced over.

One day, shortly before she left school, she met Sister Imelda in the corridor leading to the chapel. The nun said how short the years seemed since Jane's arrival at the convent. Jane stared at her feet and said nothing. Suddenly Sister Imelda asked her, 'Are you happy, Jane?' Slowly the girl raised her head.

'Happy? No. I have no one and I have nothing. Why should I be happy?'

'You have God, child.'

'Yes,' she said dully, 'I still have God.'

'And you have your youth.'

Jane paused. She wanted to tell the truth: to say that her youth had been nothing to her but a wearisome burden. It had meant a lack of independence; frustration and a need to accept that the power to control her own life and destiny was not yet hers. But she would have that power, and would have it soon, so she lowered her gaze to her feet again.

'Youth,' she said demurely, 'Yes, I still have my youth.'

On leaving school, Jane took a job in a city-centre office. At first she assumed that she would be expected to find a home for herself, and that her aunt would sever the last tenuous links. So it was a great surprise when her aunt politely asked Jane to live with her. Jane was about to refuse, but then she stopped to consider the alternatives. Her relief at leaving school was tempered with a certain fear, for much as she hated the routine of life at the convent, its very monotony had given her a feeling of security. She knew that the society of her aunt would be the nearest thing she could find to that curious combination of close physical proximity and emotional distance which she had been used to at school.

Jane therefore agreed to move back into the white attic on a permanent basis. She would pay a fixed rent and maintain her independence; and her aunt was all compliance. This made Jane most suspicious. Before long she had guessed the reason for her aunt's behaviour: her aunt did not believe that Jane would ever leave her. She felt quite sure that unless she severely antagonized her niece she would have her to care for her in her old age; and so she pretended to be docile. And when Jane understood this she knew that time would prove one or other woman to be right. She felt sure that it would be she.

But as time passed, she began instead to wonder if it would not be her aunt. Her independent working life did not fulfil any of the hopes which she had built around it; and before long she had slipped into a routine as narrow and as tedious as anything she had ever experienced at school. The office where she worked was cramped and dark; the tasks which she was given to do were simple and boring. She felt much more uncomfortable with her colleagues in the office than she had ever done with the girls in school. Often when she walked into a room silence would fall and she knew that they had been talking about her. Sometimes when she was bent over her desk she could feel the eyes of her fellow workers watching her. They thought her very odd: thought her cold and unfriendly. Some of the girls were even a little afraid of her. Certainly she had not been popular at school, but to a degree she had been understood and accepted there. Most of her schoolfellows had known her since the age of five, and having grown up with her oddness, took it for granted. They also, she now realized, had forgiven her much because she was an orphan.

At this stage in her life Jane dressed badly, the inevitable result of a life spent in uniform. The ugly gymslip of heavy bottle-green worsted which she wore when she was five was, apart from size, identical to the one which she wore when she was eighteen. She remarked upon this one day to one of the girls in the office. The girl was puzzled.

'But why did your mother send you off to boarding school when you were so small?' It was the opening Jane needed, and with the same apparent artlessness which she had employed so many times before this, she told the girl about her unhappy childhood. The anecdotes had, of course, the desired effect: the girl was shocked and deeply sympathetic; she in turn told the other girls in the office and from that time on they were kinder to Jane, and more understanding.

But this, Jane discovered, was not enough. She was very lonely now, and wanted friendship, not pity, but did not know how to break through the careful mask which she had constructed throughout her childhood. Because she felt that she could blame no one but herself for this, her misery was compounded with guilt. In her early youth she had always had an unswerving faith that there would be a happy ending, and that she would find a contentment which would vindicate all this suffering, but now she had to confront reality. Her life was simply a life, not a fairy-tale or a romantic novel, and it was perfectly possible to live long – to live all one's life – never knowing anything but futility and misery. The intensity of her loneliness frightened her.

The months and even years passed, and little changed, except that she began to have two recurring dreams. In the first dream she was trapped alone in an empty room. The walls, ceiling and floor were all painted white, and the room was harshly illuminated by artificial light. The only door was locked, and through the tightly sealed windows she could see people passing by. In the dream she felt that she had lived through a whole day, in the course of which she never ceased to beat against the windows, screaming and crying in ever-increasing panic, afraid that she would not be seen and rescued before darkness fell. But the people on the other side of the glass either did not see her, or, seeing her, they did not care, and when night came she was still always trapped alone in the room. And now, although she could not see the people she felt that they, out there in the darkness, were all gathered round to look at her. In silence they watched her, with derision and contempt and a total want of pity. Now when she stood by the windows of the brightly lit room she could see nothing out there in the night, nothing but her own hated face reflected back to her from the black glass.

In the second dream she was again locked in a room, but this time there was complete darkness and she was not alone. Although she could not see or hear anyone, she could sense another person there with her. In her dream she tried to find this person, and so for hours she felt her way around the room, searching blindly. Her outstretched hands grasped at the dark and empty air: sometimes she felt that she had been eluded by no more than a fraction of a second; sometimes she found that she was stumbling against the walls of the room. And yet her conviction that the other person *was* there never wavered. As the dream progressed her fear that she would not succeed increased, bringing her to a terrible pitch of frustration. Just when she felt that she could not bear the loneliness for a moment longer she would awake in tears.

One night, some three years after she had started work, Jane left the office in the company of one of the other girls, and as they walked along the pavement the girl suddenly stopped short before a shop window.

'Oh, look at that,' she said. 'Isn't that beautiful?' Her eye had been caught by a wedding dress of white watered silk, frothed at the neck with lace and artfully lit to show at its best the sheen of the silk.

'I wish I needed a dress like that,' said the girl wistfully. 'I'd love to be married. Wouldn't you love to be married, Jane?'

Jane was still looking at the dress, conscious of the exaggerated shape of the dummy upon which it was draped, the bust too big and the waist too narrow to be natural. She imagined a row of clothes pegs running down the dummy's back, nipping in the excess material.

'No,' she said at last. 'I don't think that I would like that.'

'What do you want, Jane?'

'I don't think that I really know,' she said, moving away from the window. She did not speak again after that, except to say 'Goodbye' when she parted from the girl.

Shortly after that she began to develop sharp physical pains which apparently had no organic cause, but would strike at any time and in any part of her body. On several occasions she fainted.

Then came the night which was to change her whole life. Standing in her aunt's chilly bathroom she suddenly caught sight of her own naked body reflected in a tilted cheval glass. She was shocked because she saw it first distantly and objectively, as if it belonged to someone else, and then she knew that in that thought there was a wish and a refusal, knew, too, that it was foolish. That strange woman's body with its breasts and the dark triangle of hair; that body, with all its implied, attendant feelings, that body, bare as a corpse, was hers, and she had to claim it. But she could not bear to look and she turned away horrified. Now you have to choose. The bath brimmed invitingly, squat upon its four clawed feet of iron. She looked away again, saw the light socket and began to cry; took a few steps towards the bath and as she wiped her eyes felt a softness and warmth in her hand which she did not want to feel; then again glimpsed her body in the mirror and saw a certain beauty which she did not want to see. She cried aloud and suddenly her whole life opened up before her: not her past life, as was supposed to happen at this particular moment, but her future life, and she saw in it a blankness and a mystery. Time would fill those empty years with something and if she now fulfilled her intention she would never know how it was all really meant to end. 'But how can I bear to live all those years?' she thought. She closed her eyes and put her hands across her face; again she cried and cried. But then she made her choice: then she said yes. Slowly she put on her nightdress. She drained the bath, put out the light, and she went to bed.

In the following weeks the pains and the two dreams about the dark room and the bright room continued, but her life was different because, for the first time since her school-days, she had a real hope that the future would be better. Her strong will reasserted itself to ensure that this would be so.

It was a few months after that night that she met the man who was later to be her husband. She was in the habit of calling into a café on her way home from work, and one day an excessive crowd had forced them, strangers, to share a table. For the first fifteen minutes she pretended to gaze into the middle distance, while in reality she was carefully studying his reflection in a mirror which hung on the opposite wall. He was covertly staring at Jane (which she, of course, clearly saw in the mirror). She guessed that he was from the country, and when the waitress came to take his order his accent proved her right. She also guessed that he was shy, and was right in that too, for when she at last asked him to pass the sugar he was startled, and he blushed. Looking at her teacup she timidly engaged him in idle conversation. She would not let him go. From long, linked, insinuating sentences she made a web of talk which communicated nothing but which held him there, listening until she had created the right moment. Then she told him about her childhood: the fire; her aunt; the hospital; the convent. She told her story as though it had all happened to someone else, and told it so well that he could not fail to be moved. When she had drawn from him all the pity she wanted she lightly changed the subject; but still she kept talking, until again she felt (and this was more dangerous) that she had created the right moment. Then she stood up, and drew the conversation shyly, clumsily, to a close, as she gathered together her jacket and handbag.

Hastily he asked if he might meet her again. She looked surprised, and became quite flustered. But said, 'Yes.'

They did meet again, and often. His home was over an hour from the city by car, and she was flattered to think of his travelling all that distance just to see her. He took her to the cinema, they went out to tea, they went walking in the park. In the course of these meetings she found out a little more about him. He told her that he lived in a farmhouse right by the lough's shore. Like Jane, he was an only child; and he lived alone with his father, his mother having died some five years before.

Soon her whole life had dwindled to an empty space flanked on one side by recent memories of being in his company, and on the other by anticipation of seeing him again in the near future.

She had a deep contempt for all those who had known from birth what it was to be loved. She did not believe that they could ever know how strange and wonderful it was to watch another person gradually fall in love with them. She certainly watched James, and watched him with a steady fascination, as a naturalist might watch a butterfly uncrumple itself from a chrysalis, or wiltingly die in a killing jar. She would always make a point of arriving early for their meetings, so that she could conceal herself at a distance and covertly watch him arrive and then pace the street disconsolately, looking at his watch, as he waited for her. Then she would leave her hiding place and approach him, her eye steadily fixed on his, so that she would not miss the moment when he caught sight of her. Because to see that moment was the whole point of the exercise: to see his face change, to see the relief and the tenderness and the love with which the mere sight of her filled him was the highlight of the entire evening. It made her feel dizzy with power.

The thought that there was something quite basically wrong with the relationship did drift into her mind occasionally, but she always quashed it. But she noticed, for example, that often when the girls at work asked her questions about James – even simple factual questions – she did not know the answers. At first she admitted her ignorance, but the longer she knew him the more embarrassing this became. Soon, she began to reply with plausible lies. It did not worry her unduly, because, she reasoned, if she did not know much about him, there was also much which he did not know about her (and, she realized, that she did not want him to know).

One night she awoke in the white attic out of a dreamless sleep. Because it was summer the room was not perfectly dark, and she could easily distinguish the shapes of the simple furniture.

She had now known James for six months, and she began to think how happy he had made her. The very night before she met him she had awoken in this same room in great distress because of a dream: now, however, she was completely at peace. She felt now that it was as if she had lived all her life looking into the disturbed waters of a rock pool, and seeing nothing because the waters were clouded with sand. But then, when she had least expected it, the surface had been stilled and the pool became clear, so that she could see into its depths where a small yellow crab moved sideways over the ribbed sand, and a few little fish glittered and were gone. Scattered on the bed of the pool were smooth black and white stones which puckered the sand where they lay, and above all this she could see her own face, reflected so perfectly that her countenance appeared to become a part of the water. Nothing could be more desirable than to stay looking into that pool for the rest of her life.

But what if the waters were to become disturbed again? Then she felt an even worse panic: she felt now that if James went out of her life everything would be lost. A few evenings after that she met him again and they went walking in the park at dusk.

'What did you first see in me, James?' she asked with feigned levity as they passed through the gates. 'Was it pity for the poor orphan?'

'No,' he said, but he said nothing more, and although he smiled he also looked embarrassed. Jane was afraid to ask why.

The park was deserted: the very light had gone from the air and from the earth, although the sky was still bright blue. Clumps of white flowers seemed to glow luminous in the parterres. Eventually they came to a deserted bandstand which loomed up in the gloom like a vast, empty gazebo, giving the surroundings the air of a large private estate rather than a public park. Together they mounted the steps and as they stood there Jane tried to imagine the place flooded with light and full of rich brassy music; but her imagination was powerless to overcome the still, scented, silent dusk in which they stood. Within the bandstand there was a wonderful sense of air contained. She felt as if they had gone into a huge, ornamental birdcage from which a few of the bars had been removed, and as she leaned back to look at the panels of white wood in the dome of the roof she felt his hand close over hers. She looked down again and he put his arms around her, and she embraced him in response. They stood for some moments, she leaning against him, silently willing him to ask her now. But when he did say 'Marry me' she did not answer at once but waited until he asked her again.

She did not look at him: her gaze was directed out and away across the park when she at last said 'Yes.'

The following week he took her to visit the farm. On seeing the house Jane immediately knew certain things as if they had been spoken to her by a prophet. She knew that she had come to her home. She knew that she would live her life out in the big grey house; and yet she knew that she would always be an outsider. Despite James's love for her, she would never love this place and it would never love her. Never, in leaving it, would she feel anything more than indifference, and she would feel no regret to close her eyes upon it either in sleep or in death.

The lough frightened her. She thought that it would be strange to live by such a huge expanse of water, where so many wild things lived; all the birds, the fish, the eels; a place strange as a forest. She wondered if she would ever become used to sleeping and waking with the knowledge that that big natural thing was out there. She could have no power over it, but it could, perhaps, have power over her, as it did over James, who could not countenance living far from water, far from the lough. There was an ease about him in the country which she had never seen in the city.

The first thing she had noticed that afternoon on stepping from the car was not the expected silence but the sound of the birds, their weird cries going on and on. They said that you could get used to anything in time. She wondered if it were true.

He brought her into the parlour, and she guessed that nothing in it had been changed since his mother's death. In the dimness she could see a fat sofa like a recumbent animal, and a small glass-fronted cabinet filled with china and trinkets. On the mantelpiece were two empty vases made of dark red glass, their rims gilded; and on the wall was a framed print of overblown, unnatural-looking roses. Heavy brown velvet curtains obscured most of the light. There was a damp, musty smell and even though it was obviously kept as a best room, it had a great air of indifference and neglect.

James led her over to the window and pointed across a flat

vista of fields, which stretched away beyond the edge of a dark orchard.

'We own all that land,' he said, 'right down to the lough shore. Almost a hundred acres we have now.' But Jane was not interested in land ownership, nor did she understand the emphasis which country people put upon it. Secretly she thought it foolish to pride oneself upon the possession of fields: one might as well point at a cloud and say 'That's mine', as far as she was concerned. She murmured politely, and then indicated a cottage which stood down near the water's edge. 'And do you own that too?'

'No,' he said, 'that's not ours. That belongs to the woman who lives there.'

'Who's she?'

'She's called Ellen,' he said, and he did not elaborate, but Jane remained silent until he added, 'She's a music teacher.'

'Has she always lived there?'

'More or less.'

'You must be very close friends,' she said, hoping for a denial, but he said rather absently, 'Yes, we are. She's been like a sister to me. I'm sure you'll get on well with her.'

'Perhaps.' Jane moved away from the window.

From the dim, slightly dank parlour, he led her through the hallway where a grandfather clock stood like an upended coffin, and into the kitchen. There, he introduced her to his elderly father who was sitting in an old broken-down armchair wedged in by the side of an Aga. On the other side of the stove there was a cardboard box containing a little lamb whose mother had died, and which James was rearing by hand. The whole house, Jane thought, was drab and uncomfortable. The kitchen smelt of sheep and tobacco. Its wall were painted half wine-red and half brown; and the cold terrazzo tiles beneath their feet were flecked white, ginger and black.

James's father seemed to like her. They talked together while James made tea, moving between the stove and a little back scullery as he did so, and all the while she secretly watched him.

When the tea was ready he served it, together with slices of bought Angel Cake, and as they ate and drank and talked there was a feeling of peace in the room. She watched James watching his father as the old man broke the pastel-coloured cake into squares and nibbled at them. The resemblance between father and son was remarkable. She felt that she could cry with relief, having at last found a circle of affection which would open and take her in.

Afterwards, when they carried the tea things through to the back scullery, James said to Jane, 'There's something here which I want to show you. Look. Quietly now, or you'll startle her.'

He pointed to a cardboard carton which had a grill from the oven placed over the top to form a makeshift cage. She peered through the bars and saw a scrap of an old jumper, and a little dish of milk, and there, huddled in a corner of the box, was a tiny robin. She gasped. The bird was so very near, its brown eyes burning and fine-feathered breast quivering. It seemed electric with life; so small, so still, but charged with an unstable energy.

But then she saw that the bird was wounded, its right wing hanging at a painful angle from its body.

'The creature!' she murmured. 'What happened to it?'

'It's my fault,' he said sadly. 'There was a rat in the shed outside and it was eating the meal, so I set a trap to catch it. But this morning when the door was open the bird flew in and ate the food I had set. The trap caught her on the wing. I hope she comes all right.' He peered in anxiously at the bird in the box, and as Jane stood up to allow him space to look more closely, she glimpsed a shadow at the scullery window.

'Who's that?' she asked James. He turned and looked.

'Oh, that's Gerald,' he said vaguely. 'He's the farm hand. We only hired him a few months ago.' He dropped his voice. 'What with Daddy getting on a bit I thought we could do with the help.' He turned his attention again to the robin, but when he straightened up some moments later, Jane was still looking out of the window at the farm hand.

Afterwards, they went back to the dingy parlour, and when they heard the outer door close behind James's father, James put his arm around her waist and pulled her to him. Jane leaned against his shoulder, conscious of the musty smell in the room and thought, 'I'll change those curtains: brown velvet's too much in here.' She could hear the ticking of the clock in the hall; but she felt that she was caught in a space and a stillness which was beyond time, so that every tick was not another second, but the same second repeated, and repeated. She kissed him, drew away, kissed him again, and then rested her face upon his shoulder.

She could hear the wild birds clearly as they cried out over the water.

CHAPTER TWO

She can hear the wild birds clearly as they cry out over the water.

It is early afternoon on the feast of the Epiphany, and Catherine and Sarah are in the parlour, dismantling the Christmas tree and putting away the decorations for another year. Catherine, rather, busies herself with the tree while her twin has by now moved over to the window, where she stands idle. She made her contribution by collecting all the sprays of holly from behind the picture frames and mirrors and then burning them in the fire which Catherine had stoked up earlier.

It is now little over a month since the cold, wet day when Sarah gathered the holly, a day recorded in her diary with a little inked star. She remembers how she hacked it from the hedge. The leaves had been glossy and dark and the fleshy berries plump and rich and as bright as blood; but now the leaves are dry and have faded in colour to olive-drab; the berries have become shrivelled by the heat of the house. As she pressed the branches down into the flames she felt sad to watch the pale dead branches burn, and the dry leaves crackle and blister and blacken, and so she turned from the fire and crossed to the window where she now stands, looking out from the warm, untidy room into the cold landscape.

A few days after Christmas, heavy snow had fallen. Its first effect had been magical, for it fell straight down on a windless night and covered everything, absolutely everything down to the smallest leaf with a crust of airy snow which held the light and sparkled. Late on the last day of December more snow had fallen. Sarah dreaded the start of the new year, and shortly before midnight she had gone out across the farmyard and had leaned back against the gate to look up at the sky.

January began while she was looking up at the snowflakes,

and admiring them as they silently fell in the moonlight, cold, countless, beautiful. It reminded her of summer when the mayflies swarmed. The nights then were warm and clear and the little grey flies formed a living grey snow which was not silent and which did not fall, but hummed horribly and trapped her as if in a pillar of cloud. The mayflies were like one of the plagues with which the God of Israel cursed Egypt, and as she thought of summer she looked up even more ardently at the snowflakes drifting noiselessly in the cold air, and she told herself, 'Cherish this.'

It was foolish to long for the summer to come.

At its first falling the snow was beautiful, but the first days of the new year have now passed, and no more has fallen. The thaw has not begun, but the snow has gone from the roofs of the buildings, from plants and from branches, so that the trees in the orchard are now all black against the sky and the snow no longer sparkles but looks dull, unreflective and damp. Sarah looks past the edge of the dark orchard and across the level fields which stretch beyond it, to the little cottage which stands near the lough shore. She looks long and intently, pretending not to hear and trying not to think about the pronounced wheeze of her sister's breath as she steadily works. Instead, she tries to concentrate upon the desolate sound of the wild birds.

This is her home.

The great sense of space given by the wide sky and the flatness of the land is belied everywhere by the melancholy want of colour. Now she is literally seeing the place in its true colours, for the brightness of spring will be spurious in an area which is truly sad, drab, and dead. If you have been born here you can never belong elsewhere. If you have been born elsewhere, you can never belong here. Sarah knows that she is trapped. Now, as she stands by the window, she feels unspeakably sad. Why, on this winter's afternoon, should she feel so strongly that everything is ending? The year has barely begun, but she knows that it is foolish to expect that it will bring any hope; that it is always foolish to expect too much from the simple passage of time.

She is glad that Christmas is over, for it is a feast which she has never liked. Even as a child it was always a disappointment to her. She does not turn around – she does not need to – to see the decorations which will be stored in the attic until the following December. Their mother had bought these decorations when the sisters were tiny. In later years they always intended to buy some fresh ones and throw away the most bedraggled of the strands of tinsel, and the most tarnished of the little gilt stars. But each year comes and goes and the same decorations adorn the tree year after year after year. By virtue of this it has become timeless, and the little Christmas tree with its strange apples of chill, pastel-coloured glass is as eternal as the trees in the orchard with their unfailing cycle of bud, blossom and fruit. Sarah does not turn around to look at the decorations for she remembers them all.

Catherine, on the other hand, forgets everything. Every year she forgets about the little elves whose bodies are made of pine cones, forgets the Chinese lanterns of coloured tissue paper. She cannot remember details of texture, colour, dimension and smell. Sarah cannot understand the way in which her sister's mind works, nor indeed the way in which her whole life operates, when every experience becomes so quickly and so absolutely a thing of the past: a dead thing. It is even tempting to think that she has forgotten her disappointment of the autumn: but that is surely too much to expect. For a moment, Sarah allows herself to think of her sister's life and of her future, and she feels a great sense of pity.

Because of her bad memory, Catherine keeps a diary, stout as a ledger, with marbled endpapers. In this she contains her past. Sarah now thinks that it is a good idea to keep a diary as comprehensive as this, for it gives Catherine a degree of power over her life. Leaning her head against the glass she thinks, *Perhaps tonight I ought to write all this down, I too ought to try to recreate this afternoon on paper, and contain it all: the fire, the holly, the tree, the snow: and Catherine.*

But even as she thinks this she knows that it is foolish to struggle against the passage of time. When Sarah thinks about the future she feels great confusion, and even greater fear.

'Sarah?'

'Yes?'

'Give me a hand with these boxes, please.'

Sarah pauses for a moment before turning away from the window, and when she does she studiously avoids looking her sister in the eye. As she bends to pick up a box she does not see how sad Catherine is as she looks down at her, and even if she did see she would not understand.

Catherine wishes that Sarah would not go to the cottage that afternoon, and wishes that she could say, 'Please don't go – don't ever go again – stay here with me instead,' and that her sister would comply without asking for reasons.

That same morning Catherine herself had been obliged to go to the cottage with a letter which had been brought in error to the farmhouse. The scene comes back to her vividly now and she is again at the cottage door. Ellen is making tea and insists that Catherine join her. She does so with great reluctance. From behind the closed door of the parlour comes the soft, tinny sound of a Chopin Nocturne being played with merely technical competence on an old piano. Humming gently to this, Ellen pours the weak, golden tea into two cups which are so thin and translucent that Catherine can see the china darken as the level of the tea rises.

Inwardly she sneers at their excessive gentility: Ellen with her toy cups and her paper doilies and her linen napkins and her china-handled cake slice: grounds for contempt, perhaps, but nothing more. Yet what Catherine feels towards Ellen is much stronger than contempt. Paper doilies are far too light to hold the weight of hatred. She watches Ellen over the rim of her teacup, and suddenly she realizes the strangeness of the situation. For here she is, quietly drinking tea with a woman whom she would happily see damned. An eternity of outer darkness scarcely seems adequate punishment for Ellen, and Catherine can think of no suffering from which she would spare her if it lay within her power to do so.

Catherine then remembers that she truly wants to be good:

but when this hatred of Ellen comes over her, she feels as if a black, dreadful flower is opening in her heart. Her capacity for hatred fills her with awe. But it is her duty to forgive. *If I were to die now,* Catherine thinks, *I too would deserve damnation.*

'Do you feel all right, dear?'

'Yes.'

Catherine sips the tea and takes a slice of cake from the plate which Ellen holds out to her, but she only crumbles the cake in her fingers, for she cannot eat it. As they sit there listening to the music from the parlour she imagines Peter's fingers, his clean square-nailed fingers pressing down softly on the cool piano keys. She knows that above the piano there is a photograph of Ellen's wedding, and she is glad that she does not have to look at it. Catherine has never been able to understand why her mother loaned Ellen her wedding dress. She knows that she flatly refused to be her matron of honour. Catherine and Sarah's father had been best man at the wedding, and in the parlour photograph there is a shadow on the groom. The dress and the marked resemblance which Ellen bore to Jane, the mother of the two girls, makes the photograph look uncannily like the pictures which they have of their own mother's wedding. Catherine feels that she could not bear to look at that photograph now, it hurts her deeply even to think about it.

Suddenly Ellen says, 'I suppose that you still miss your mother a great deal?' Catherine feels tears come to her eyes and she hopes that Ellen knows they are caused by anger and hatred rather than grief. She turns her head aside and she does not speak. Ellen also remains silent, and for a moment Catherine thinks, *She must suffer too,* but she quashes this thought at once. She does not want to feel any compassion for the woman.

The music draws to a gentle conclusion, and after a moment's pause the parlour door squeaks softly open. Peter enters hesitantly. 'I heard voices,' he says, 'I thought it was Sarah.'

You mean you were afraid it was Sarah, Catherine thinks, and she wants to say aloud, 'No, but doubtless she'll be over later,' a temptation which she resists with difficulty.

'We were just speaking of Sarah and Catherine's mother. The girl's the image of her, isn't she?'

'Remarkable likeness,' says Peter, not smiling and not greeting Catherine, in fact barely glancing at her as he cuts a slice of cake for himself. Catherine correctly recognizes the words as a veiled insult, for she knows that Peter disliked her mother, finding her distant and cold, and he thinks that Catherine is in the same mould.

'Now Sarah's a different matter altogether,' Ellen begins, but Catherine interrupts her rudely.

'We're twins,' she flatly says. 'Identical twins.'

Ellen purses her lips and then says coldly, 'Well, yes. I suppose you are . . . in some respects.'

Catherine rises to her feet. 'I must be going,' she says, and in her haste to leave she almost shatters the frail little teacup. She knows that her departure is too abrupt to be politic; and in the last look Ellen gives her there is both bafflement and barely veiled hostility.

Now Catherine wonders nervously if Peter will mention her odd behaviour to Sarah when she goes to the cottage that afternoon. She knows that Sarah will go, for even as they lift the boxes to carry them upstairs for storage, Catherine sees her sister look out of the window again, and then glance at her watch.

A short time later, Sarah stands by her bedroom window watching the cottage. Every Saturday afternoon Ellen goes to the next town where she spends some hours giving music lessons in a rented room. Sarah waits patiently, as she waits every week for Ellen's departure. As she stands there she idly takes in her hand the tiger cowrie shell which Peter gave to her as a Christmas gift. Bright, smooth, cold as a stone, she turns it over in her hand and watches it catch the light, then strokes it gently against her face. She likes the colours: soft and dark and dun, yet still it is hard and bright.

She finds it hard to believe that this is a natural object, a thing from the sea; hard to believe that there are places where such things can be picked up along the shoreline. She looks at the shell and thinks, *What have we to touch this*? The image of a gull's egg drifts unbidden into her mind. Once they had gathered gulls' eggs out on an island, and she remembers them vividly: dun, like the cowrie, but duller, frailer, and weighty with the life of the bird within. She sets the sea shell on the window-sill and she folds her arms.

She hates her eagerness to go to the cottage. Week by week the importance of these visits has grown, until now they are the only things which make her life bearable. She wishes this were not the case. She knows that Peter does not realize how desperately she needs to visit him every week. While she resents his obtuse failure to see this, she is relieved too, for she knows that as soon as he notices her dependence he will also realize the power which he has to control her happiness. She fears and dreads that.

He must know that she will come to him that afternoon, for she goes without fail, and she wishes that for once she had the courage to stay at home. But even as she thinks this she sees the door of the cottage open, and Ellen comes out, bundled up against the cold and carrying a flat music case of tan leather. And as soon as Sarah sees this, she goes from the room to fetch her overcoat and boots.

Unlike her sister, Sarah loves the little cottage in which so little has changed over the years. The bobbled red cloth across the overmantel, the long brass fire-irons lying in the fender, the curtains of heavy silk and the tiny china cups: all these she remembers from her childhood. The self-consciously gentrified air of the place appeals to her, and she is glad of the absence of all things concerning farm life. Looking over to the window when she enters, she sees a table stacked with blue-backed school exercise books.

'Am I disturbing you?' she asks.

'No, not at all,' he says. 'I can mark these later.'

Smiling, she walks across the room, puts her arms around him and kisses him.

The windows of the cottage are small, and the weak rays of

the January sun barely penetrate the low-ceilinged room. The only other sources of light are a desk lamp and a small red lamp which burns perpetually before an oleograph of the Sacred Heart. Sarah can never become used to such pictures. Her mother strongly disapproved of them, and taught her children to pray before a candle or some flowers. Sarah cannot believe in a doe-eyed God whose hair curls prettily at the nape of his neck. At best, she finds such pictures foolish, meaningless or odd; at worst, she finds them shocking, and she wonders how people can live out their daily lives beneath them, seeing every day the wounds and the blood.

She remembers visiting the cottage as a child, and then too the picture had been a frightful mystery to her; then too the visits had been clandestine. Her parents had never forbidden her to call on Ellen and Peter, but they had not approved of such visits either. When Ellen gave her an apple or a bun she had always known to hide or eat the evidence before going home. The kindness of such gifts was never appreciated by her parents, and to this day she cannot understand why. Since her mother's death her father has been too sad or distracted to notice or care what Sarah does, but Catherine, she realizes, seems to be trying to supplant their parents. Sarah knows that her sister has always been uncomfortable in Ellen's company. She had once thought it no more than an unreasoned habit which she had picked up from her mother. But Sarah has felt this disapproval strengthen since the summer of their mother's death, more than two years ago. It is as if Catherine wants to draw her back from any possible involvement outside the family, and just as she thinks this Peter says, 'Your sister was over here this morning.'

'Oh?'

'Yes. She brought a letter. Sarah – is there anything wrong with Catherine?'

She immediately moves away from him and says, 'Wrong? What do you mean, wrong?'

'I don't know,' he says, embarrassed now. 'She just seemed a little . . . strange, and I wondered if something was wrong.'

'Perhaps you read too much into what my sister says and does simply because you don't like her.'

He opens his mouth to deny this, but she looks at him angrily and turns her back on him. They stand in silence.

After a few awkward moments she turns to him again and says politely, 'How's school?'

'Fine,' he replies, and then he begins to tell her in some detail of how his teaching is progressing. It is three days now since the beginning of the new term, and Sarah only half listens to his lies. No matter what he says she knows that he hates teaching as much as she hates working on the farm. Once he was more honest: while still at teacher-training college he often told her that he doubted his capacity to be a good teacher. But since mid-December, when their friendship changed, they are both less likely to tell the truth when they are talking to each other, and she feels a reserve, almost a politeness between them which is becoming worse each week. It increases in direct proportion to the degree of physical intimacy reached; and she thinks of the day when they will talk about the weather. But when Peter asks her what she is thinking of, and why she is smiling, she does not answer him. Instead, she once more crosses the room and kisses him. After some moments he says to her very hesitantly, 'Sarah, do you . . .'

She anticipates the question, and with a deep sigh she interrupts him. 'Do I what?' she says wearily, and this time it is he who draws away from her.

'Nothing,' he says sulkily. 'It doesn't matter.'

'Make me some tea, then,' she says.

She follows him into the kitchen and as they wait for the kettle to boil Peter gazes out of the window at the dark lough. At last he speaks, almost as if he were thinking out loud in an empty room, and he says, 'A more cruel creature than you never existed.'

'No,' she says, in a voice as soft and disinterested as his own.

'No, I don't suppose they come much worse than me.' There is another moment's pause, and then they simultaneously look at each other and smile.

But a short while later as they sit in the parlour drinking tea she thinks seriously, *I am very cruel: I am.* When she looks across at Peter she knows that she is guilty, and she wonders if he feels used. She wishes that she could feel a genuine interest in his life and well-being, wishes that she could bring herself to confide in him. It would be for his sake alone, not hers: such confidence would give him a sense of being trusted.

But where to begin? With her mother? It would be good, she thinks, looking at him steadily, if she could bring herself to speak of the time of her mother's death. Would he be shocked or sympathetic if she told him the truth? The death had been sudden, and for the first few days Sarah had been grieved and stunned. Every morning when she awoke the loss of her mother had been the first thought in her mind, and she now remembers how incongruous simple things had been: the sound of the wild birds crying out over the lough; the way the morning light lay dappled on the pillow and quilt; the sweet intimate smell of the sheets: to lie quietly in bed and think that these things, and that every other little thing in a house as familiar to her as her own body had not changed, but that one great change had been permitted – that her mother had died and would never be seen in the house again – had seemed shocking to her. It was an affront to reality.

On those first mornings she lay and felt grief descend like a great weight upon her heart and mind, and she knew that throughout the day ahead that grief, that heaviness would still be there, made worse by the sight of her father's suffering. He could hardly bear the loss of his wife, and it frightened Sarah to see him suffer so much.

And then, amazingly, on the fifth day after the death, she awoke in the morning to the exact converse of these feelings, for she felt relief and a great sense of lightness, as though some terrible constraint had been lifted from her. Rolling over in bed, she had whispered into the pillow, 'Thank God she's dead.'

Throughout the following day she could scarcely hide her happiness, and Catherine was shocked when she found her sister humming pleasantly to herself as she sifted through the letters of sympathy. After that, Sarah had tried to be more discreet, but she found it difficult to contain these feelings, and she tried to explain them to herself. 'I did love Mama,' she thought, 'I did, I did.' But only now when her mother was safely dead could she admit to the knowledge which qualified that; she had been afraid of her too, and had often even hated her for her cold self-possession. She had been quietly scornful of anyone who fell short of her own level of self-sufficiency. Against the sadness of loss Sarah had to set the honest relief of knowing that her mother would never again sit there, pretending to read or knit or do a crossword, while secretly watching every move her daughters made, watching and silently judging. All her life, Sarah now saw, had been an unconscious struggle against her mother, for she had been afraid that she would grow up to be just like her: just as cold, just as calculating and just as self-contained. Perhaps if she had lived she would have beaten Sarah and made of her what she wanted; but her death was her failure, her death gave victory to her daughter. Sarah could not feel or even imagine her mother's spiritual presence after her death, nor did she want to. She even found it hard at times to take seriously the great grief of her father and sister and often she wanted to say to them, 'Can't you see that this is for the best? We will get over the loss of her, and we'll be much happier without her than we ever were with her.' But she could never bring herself to speak like this until one afternoon when she and Catherine were standing by their mother's grave. Catherine cried while her sister looked indifferently at the fresh dark earth and the fading flowers, and suddenly she heard her own voice say, 'I don't care that she's dead. We're not. We're alive.'

But if her mother did not defeat her, and had not made of her the monster she wanted, why has Sarah come to the cottage today? Why does she come every week? To confide in Peter would be to admit that she still has something to prove and, what is worse, that she is using him to prove it. As awareness of this breaks over her she feels deeply ashamed: nothing could be lower than to use another person's love to bolster up one's own faults, and she feels no love for Peter, only a mild fear that he will one day discover how little he means to her. And the thought now comes to her, quite cold and objective: *I have nobody and I have nothing.* The loneliness which follows this thought is so terrifying that she hastily puts down her teacup and flings herself against Peter, clinging and crying. All along he had been watching the sadness on her face, watching and not understanding, but now he tries gently to console her, which only makes Sarah feel worse. Full of self-hatred and still sobbing she thinks, *Mama, dead as you are, I wish you were here, I wish I could believe that you're watching me now,* and very gently she presses her mouth against Peter's. After a few moments she draws away and then kisses him again.

And later, when they are sitting on the sofa with their arms around each other, Peter notices that she is gazing blankly away from him, and leaning over he whispers, 'What's wrong, Sarah? Why won't you tell me what's bothering you?'

She wishes that she could tell, but this is too dangerous for words. If she were to name this thing and talk about it she would give it definition and in some mysterious way make it real. And if she does not speak perhaps it will not be real, perhaps it will not happen, perhaps she can find some protection in silence. And there is a danger, too, that it will perhaps bring him closer.

Closing her eyes she says very quietly, 'No.'

'Please,' he urges her, 'please tell me.'

But still she refuses to look at him and again she refuses to tell. 'No,' she says, and then she adds wearily, 'Peter, you ask me too much.'

When Sarah returns to the farm that afternoon she finds Catherine in the back scullery, coughing as she ladles greasy chicken soup into a bowl of thick blue and white striped delft.

'Is that for Dada?'

'Yes.'

Catherine puts the soup, together with a plate of bread, upon the kitchen table, then calls her father in from the farmyard to eat. This done, she goes upstairs, while Sarah pretends to be busy, for the pot of tea which she makes is only an excuse to remain in the back scullery. As she waits for the kettle to boil she stands with her back against the sink and looks through the open scullery door to the kitchen where her father sits drinking the soup. When she interrupted Peter that afternoon he had been on the point of asking her if she loved him, and she almost laughs to think of it now. Love! The poor fool! What did he know about love? Little enough if he could even ask such a question. What in honesty had he expected her to say? Yes? Could even Peter's foolishness go to such a point?

Sarah has only ever loved her family, and her family has made her suffer. Looking through the open door to where her father is sitting is like looking into a seashell which is coiled and chambered. Each chamber is a memory, its size and brightness in accordance with its position on the coil of time which stops with the shell's sharp apex: the moment of her birth. But beyond that there is a wide yellow shore scattered with shells, and she can see but she cannot touch the huge shells which contain her father's secret memories. She cannot imagine what it would be like to move through those vast coiled systems of chambers, seeing with her father's eyes the eighteen years which make the sum total of her own brief life, and then before that those early, mysterious years which lie beyond the scope of Sarah's memories: the years of her parents' marriage prior to the birth of their children; the years of his life before his marriage, spent on the farm alone with his father; the years of his boyhood and youth spent with both his parents, prior to his mother's death, and then these shells also come to the still point of his birth and are ended. But before this were the lives and memories of his parents, and their parents before that, and their parents before that: the shells of these memories have been sucked back into the sea by the tide, and some have been dashed by waves against the rocks and have been broken; some have fallen to the sandy bed of the sea, and some will drift forever and forever. And Mama: she wonders what has happened to the poor misshapen shell of her mother's life, and she wishes that she could have saved it above all from the cold blue infinite sea.

Now, on this winter's evening, she has to force herself to look from the back scullery up into the kitchen, and force herself to go into each chamber of her memory. She goes first to the kitchen where her father now sits alone, drinking his soup, and then she goes beyond it to the times when he sits alone in the same empty kitchen far into the night. He has developed this habit since his wife's death, and it saddens his daughters very much to see him so lonely. If they chance to enter and speak to him he does not reply but sits there until long after darkness has fallen. He smokes incessantly: as Catherine and Sarah go up to bed they can see from the stairs the tiny orange glow of his cigarette moving through the blackness from his hand to his mouth. In the morning when they come down they find the room filled with the smell of stale cigarettes. She remembers sadly how at first they had tried to console him, but nothing worked: they have had, at last, to abandon him to his strange refusal of all possible comfort.

Frequently on the mornings after these solitary vigils he claims that he is sick and refuses to get out of bed so that all the farm work falls to Sarah. His illness is a lie: he is too depressed to face life on those days, and too ashamed to admit it. He will not hire a farm hand, and on the days when her father cries off, Sarah is stiff and exhausted by nightfall. Once she asked him, 'What would I do if you were very ill for a long time? What if you died?' and had felt despairing when he had merely said, 'You'd carry on the farm, of course,' and would not discuss the matter further. Only on one occasion has she broken through to him on this subject, and that is another of the chambers into which she must now force herself to go. She goes back to a particular day in November: a cold and bleak day. Her father has refused to get out of bed and as usual Sarah has undertaken all the farm work alone. In the course of the day four cows break out of a field. For over an hour she searches for the animals in a thick fog and chill, seeping rain, finds them, drives them home and puts them back into the field, but as she stretches a strand of barbed wire across the gap through which they escaped the damp wire slips through her fingers and one of the barbs tears into the flesh of her wrist.

When she bursts weeping into the kitchen she finds her father there in his dressing-gown, poking disconsolately in the bread-bin, but he turns around in surprise as she enters.

'Look at it. Look at it, Dada. You did that. That's your fault.'

'Jesus Christ!' He backs into a corner, but his fear only makes her more excitable.

'Look at it! Look at the blood! This wouldn't have happened if you had been there with me. Good God,' she sobs, 'I've had as much as I can take. So you wanted a son to carry on the farm, did you, Dada? Well, hard luck, because you didn't get one, you got me and Catherine, and she's not fit for this and neither am I. Do you hear me, Dada? Are you listening? Stop trying to make a man of me. It won't work. If you want a son you may hire one from someone else.'

Perhaps this might have made him angry so that he swore at her or even struck her, but instead he puts his head in his hands and cries and cries. He makes no attempt to control his grief, but lets his cries rise to an hysterical edge which frightens his daughter. And what frightens her most of all is the altruism of it, for as he weeps she hears her own cries rise up to meet and match his grief, independent of her will, and joining to his weeping so that suddenly she does not know where her own grief ends and his begins: in the terrible noise that fills the kitchen she cannot distinguish her own cries.

'Stop that, Dada. Stop it now.' Catherine goes over to her sister and picks up her hand. 'Go and get dressed, Dada. We'll have to take her to the hospital for an anti-tetanus injection, so go now and get ready. Go!'

Still crying, he leaves the room. The two noises are prised apart, and now she can hear the distinct sobs of her father as he goes upstairs. Catherine speaks harshly to her sister as she crosses the scullery. 'Oh, you stop your miserable snivelling too, for goodness sake, and put your wrist under this.' She turns on the cold tap, and the icy water hammers noisily into the steel sink.

Obedient but wincing, Sarah holds the wound under the clear stream of water while her sister goes to fetch a bottle of antiseptic and some cotton wool. While she swabs her sister's wrist there is silence, save for the occasional sob which escapes Sarah.

'You should have known better,' Catherine says eventually, 'for you know what he's like.'

And the memory of the clinical smell of the antiseptic and the absolute silence in which they drove to the hospital takes her back to the night of her mother's death when they follow the ambulance in just such a tense silence. On arrival, they are made to sit on plastic chairs in the corridor outside the room where the doctors are working to save her. As they wait, they hear a noise: double doors at the end of the pale corridor split, and two white figures enter, pushing a bed. As they draw level with the waiting family the occupant of the bed is clearly visible. It is a little child, no more than four years old, who is dressed in white like the two figures who conduct her. She is tucked with almost mathematical precision between white, sterile sheets. On her head is a plastic hat which covers all her hair, and her wide brown eyes are steady and cold in a little face which is pale, sick and stoical. The wheels of the bed squeak as it moves along the corridor to the next set of double doors which open, close, and the bed has gone: there is nothing again. Sarah feels a pang of regret. In the few seconds while the bed passed she had something to think about, apart from the fact of her mother dying. And now that it has passed it is her father she thinks of, and not her mother. When she thinks of this night afterwards she will remember shame, not grief: shame to think that this is the first time ever she has seen her father as a man first and as her father second, the first time that she has truly considered her parents as people. She will always be ashamed to think that her mother has had to reach the point of death before her daughter is woman enough to see this. She sees the love of her father for her mother as a thing apart from her, from Sarah, and that love is mysterious and shocking as a love observed must always be. That love makes her feel lonely. Love: a word they shy away from in the family. And to think of that forces her out of that chamber of her memory, and brings her to the latest and perhaps the most painful chamber of all, for its full implications have not yet been resolved.

It is a day in summer now, in the year of their mother's death, and Catherine is standing by the kitchen window, next to a bright red geranium in a brass pot. Catherine is not looking at her sister, she is speaking slowly and snapping leaves off the geranium, withered ones to begin with but when these are all gone she continues with the fresh leaves and the blossoms, snap, snap, and Sarah is too amazed to pay any heed to this, for her sister is saying that she is going to enter a convent, she is quite decided and nothing will stop her. For a moment Sarah cannot reply, for the thought of being so parted from her sister is too much for her, so that when she does speak she has to hide the pain of this in anger.

'And what about me?' she asks. 'What about me? Am I to be abandoned here with Dada and the cattle?'

'Perhaps . . . I suppose so . . . unless you go somewhere else.' And Catherine is now caressing the brass flank of the big pot with the palm of her hand and saying, 'You must lead your own life . . . you must decide.'

Sarah is about to tell her how selfish she is when Catherine turns from the window and says fretfully, 'Oh don't scold me! Let me be! I know it's madness but what can I do? I have no real choice. I believe in God and I love Him, and you have to follow through love and belief. You know that, don't you? I can't deny what I feel, nor what I know. I mean, if you don't put your life in line with what you believe – with what you love – what's the point in living at all?'

And as Sarah remembers this now she bangs the kettle down upon the drainingboard with such force that her father glances up in surprise from the soup bowl. Love! How dare he – how *dare* Peter talk to her about love? If ever he does such a thing again she will say to him softly, 'Why yes, yes, of course. I love you,' and make him reply in kind; and then she will put her hand to his throat and she will say to him, 'So what, pray, are you going to do about it?'

Now it is night. Sarah goes to the parlour where Catherine is watching a chat show on television. Two of the guests are sisters who have lived apart for all their lives. They came to know of each other's existence only when one sister realized that the precise hour of her birth had been recorded on her birth certificate, and that she therefore probably had a twin. A long and difficult search led at last to a happy reunion. They also discovered that they have a brother who is still alive, but with whom they have not yet been reunited. And when they say this the host of the programme smiles and says that he has a surprise treat for the sisters, for the lost brother has been found, and he is here in the studio. The host invites him to come down from the audience to join his sisters, and as the orchestra plays a few bars of sentimental music and the audience clap their hands, a small man stands up in their midst. Looking nervous and a trifle apprehensive he trots down the steps to the front of the studio. His sisters stand up, and as they greet their brother there is, for the first few seconds, a feeling of formality and embarrassment, as if they cannot overcome the fact that they have been strangers for so long. The greeting is performed solely for the cameras and for the public: it is the expected thing. But in that moment when they first embrace all restraint vanishes. They put their arms around each other and they huddle tightly weeping in a knot, their backs forming a circular barrier against the world, indifferent now to the presence of the cameras, indifferent to everything but each other. As Sarah watches this she feels that she is going to cry, and she is taken aback when Catherine suddenly jumps up and turns off the television.

'I don't know why they show things like that,' she says, slowly, moodily, in the following silence. 'Things so private. It's obscene – horrible – feeding off other people's emotions. I don't know why they do it.'

In the cottage across the fields, Peter is watching the same television programme, and he is thinking of the sisters, for it reminds him of them, and he wonders if it reminds them of the same scene. For as he watches he thinks of Sarah and Catherine and James, their father, on the day of Jane's burial. They too had stood in just such a pose with their grief, locking out the rest of the world. He had made excuses to himself for his feelings, saying that the death of his own father when he was too young to remember him was at the heart of his unease. It makes him feel uncomfortable now to think of how he had then felt jealous and resentful of the family; had wanted to force his way into the circle and be locked there with them in their grief. And worse: as they stood there Catherine had been stroking her sister's back, slowly and gently moving her hand, clenching and unclenching in her fist the cloth of her sister's coat; and Peter must now admit to himself that it was while watching this that he felt for the first time an inkling of sexual desire for Sarah. Because of the circumstances Peter was immediately horrified at himself. He thought his feelings unnatural and disgusting and at once suppressed them; kept them quashed for two years. Even now he hates to consider it, and he is glad when the television programme comes to an end.

Shortly afterwards he goes to bed, resigning himself to a wakeful night, for Peter suffers from insomnia. He fears the night as a little child might do, and he fears sleep as others fear death. The bedroom will remain illuminated until morning because he is afraid of the dark. If the room had been all blackness he would have had extra fears beside the fear of sleep: foolish, irrational fears. Peter would imagine that things are coming out of the wardrobe to attack him; that cold hands will suddenly touch his brow; that pale faces will appear, smiling, unbidden, at the window. He therefore takes particular care to pull the curtains and close out the darkness, but he does not realize that light from his room is seeping out through a crack in the curtains, and he does not know that at that very moment Sarah is looking at the line of light which indicates his window. She is watching from her own bedroom window, for she, too, is just on the point of going to bed.

As she lets fall the curtain and switches on the light someone knocks gently upon the door. It is Catherine.

'Are you in bed? I don't want to disturb you. Can you lend me a pen?'

'Come in.' Sarah crosses to the dressing-table, and as she begins to rummage Catherine says, 'I have to fill in my diary.' But when Sarah finds a pen and turns to hand it to her sister (and sees how very thin she looks in her dressing-gown) Catherine starts, is confused and embarrassed, and taking the pen she says nothing but leaves the room. Sarah is puzzled by this, until she catches sight of herself in the dressing-table mirror and sees, low down on her neck, the mark of a little bite. She swears under her breath: thinks, *Well, at least now she'll have something to write in her precious diary,* and then, for the second and final time that night she puts out her light.

CHAPTER THREE

'Entreat me not to leave you or to return from following you, for where you go I will go, and where you lodge I will lodge, your people shall be my people and your God my God. Where you die I will die and there I will be buried. May the Lord do so to me and more also if even death parts me from you.'

Jane frowned beneath her veil as she listened to the first lesson and wondered if she was making a mistake, but the feeling lasted only for a moment. She was married in white before a small congregation, made smaller still by her aunt's protestation of illness on the morning of the wedding. Closing her eyes, she tried to pray. She did not think that the sacramental significance of the occasion and the smug sense of personal triumph which she felt were mutually exclusive. The girls whom she had invited from her office did not know her real motives. 'And why not me?' she had wanted to cry as she watched them pass her engagement ring from hand to incredulous hand. 'Why shouldn't I marry? Why should I be different to any other woman?' Strange, she thought, as she watched James put the plain gold ring upon her steady finger, that she should kneel in apparent white submission at such a moment.

Through all the wedding arrangements, James had expressed a strong preference in one matter alone, and that was in the choice of their honeymoon hotel. He elected that they spend a week at a particular fishing village in the north and Jane readily agreed. After arrangements had been made he remarked that it was the same hotel where his parents had spent their honeymoon.

The village was small and unfashionable, the hotel shabby. Jane suddenly felt foolish as she stood in the chilly reception, and she tried to avoid seeing her reflection in the stained mirror which hung behind the desk, for she looked too young, too thin, and overdressed in her light linen suit and her little veiled hat. The very confetti caught in her hair seemed contrived, as if she had lifted some strands with a comb and carefully arranged the little bits of coloured paper.

The middle-aged woman behind the desk betrayed the low status of the hotel by her over-familiarity. 'You look starved to death, daughter,' she said as she handed over the key. 'Once you get settled in you come down again and we'll see about getting you a nice hot cup of tea – or something stronger, if you prefer.'

But Jane drew back from such maternal solicitude, for as the woman looked at her Jane could see in her eyes something more than kindness. She saw pity: and as she turned to follow James up the stairs she had to fight the urge to go back and say to the woman, 'Keep your pity, for I neither need nor want it. Never in my life have I less needed pity than I do now.'

The little hotel was on the top of a high cliff, and the room in which James and Jane were to stay was on the seaward side of the building: perpetually they heard the sound of the waves' rumble on the beach below. The room was cold, cramped and harshly lit by an unshaded bulb which made no shadows and put into sharp relief the simple furniture. The bed was made up with sheets of hard cold linen, a bed so big that it almost filled the tiny room, and embarrassed them both. When James touched her Jane stiffened and said, 'It's too bright in here.' Drawing away from him she switched out the light. But she was unprepared for the blackness which followed: a blackness and a quietness which was strange to her, for always in the city the noise of the traffic and the rays of the yellow street lights filtered up from below.

The following morning she was brushing her hair while James dressed, and she noticed suddenly that James was looking at her. She stopped with the brush still caught in her hair, and looked at him, but she could not define what was in his stare. James looked away quickly, as if to pretend that he had not been watching her, but as she started slowly to brush her hair again he made the mistake of glancing once more in her direction, and found that she was still staring at him, her eyes steady and unperturbed. Now he was embarrassed and confused. Slowly she stood up, and crossed the room to him. Then she put up her hand and very gently she touched his shoulder as if he were something she had dreamed, and whose substantial reality she had to prove.

When they went downstairs the same motherly woman who had given them the keys of their room now served them with breakfast: two large, greasy fries, each with a soft fried egg. Jane would not eat, but sat with her eyes fixed subversively on the salt while her food grew cold and congealed before her. The woman bustled back and forth with tea and toast, chattering to James as she did so. Jane resisted all attempts by her husband to draw her into the conversation, and remained in stubborn silence. As she removed Jane's untouched plate the woman made a light remark, saying that she ought to eat better, that she needed to 'keep her strength up'. At this, Jane raised her head and fixed the woman with a cold, steady stare, full of outrage. The woman was deeply embarrassed at the idea of having given offence to the little girl on her honeymoon; and she apologized profusely. And as James accepted these apologies, 'Of course we know that you meant no offence,' Jane lifted her eyes and gave him a look which demanded that he choose sides. He fell silent. When they left the table Jane was the only one who felt any degree of satisfaction. Secretly she was proud of how, without uttering a single word, she had bested the maternal woman. The incident had shaken James too: she was glad of that.

Later that day, they went walking along the cliff top. They knelt down and saw far below them the gulls squatting on their untidy nests in cleft rocks of the cliff face. Over their heads more gulls wheeled, mean-eyed birds with stiff pink legs and plump white bodies. Caught between the sea below and the sky above; the white foam of one and the white clouds of the other; the sound of the waves below and the cries of the birds above, Jane felt a strange sense of disembodiment. She felt lonely too, and realized then that she wanted to heighten this sensation rather than defeat it. Far below them there was a little ledge. It was extremely narrow, and was accessible only by a beaten path which wound down dangerously from where they were sitting. 'I'm going down there,' she said suddenly, and as she moved to go James put his hand on her arm, tried to restrain her. She pushed him away.

Gingerly she made her way to the ledge, and she heard James calling to her to come back. She ignored him: knowing that he would be too afraid to follow her was ultimately what had made her go down the path. If her only escape that day had lain within a ring of fire, she would have stepped into it without a backward glance.

On reaching the ledge she sat down. A stiff salt breeze blew her hair across her face, she pushed it aside and looked out to the west, saw a beach: a long pale sickle of sand separating the green sea from the green land, and she thought, *I'll always remember this*. She knew then that in this thought was the significance of the scene before her. Things had once happened of which she now had no memory, but what was known could never be unknown: it could only be forgotten. As a child she had wept for the want of memories, but now she saw that they could be a curse, chaining her to the past. If only she could forget all those years of longing to remember! Now she wished passionately that she could be like a thing which had burst ignorant from an egg a second before; a thing that would live and at once forget and so be always new. What alternative was there? She raised her head and glanced up at the sun; was blinded and looked away. Perhaps to be like that: to be hidden in brightness, to be bright as God, living for eternity in unapproachable light. She wished that she could stop believing still that her parents lived in such a light. They above all were what she wanted to forget; and yet now they seemed to be everywhere, as they had been when she was a child. That presence had then been a comfort, but it was no comfort now to feel her mother's eye in the hot sun above her, or to sense her in the sea breeze or in the musty smell which emanated from the hotel's dank cupboards and clung to her clothes. *Look, then,* thought Jane fiercely. *Just look at me, I've made a life for myself after all. I'm going to be happy. I hope that you can see me for every second of every day.*

When she edged her way back up to the top of the cliff she could see at once that James was afraid and angry, but before he had time to speak she put her arms around him.

'I'm sorry,' she said, 'I promise that I'll never do anything like that again.'

They walked back holding hands, and when they reached the hotel she stopped him on the step, kissed him very tenderly and then they pushed open the glass door. They walked through the shabby hallway to the stairs, past the desk where the woman in charge of the hotel pretended not to notice them.

But that night when James told her that he loved her, and when Jane opened her mouth to reply in kind she could not say the words. No matter how much she willed herself to say it she could not; but other words came out instead.

'You're never to think that you can hide anything from me because you can't. Perhaps I don't know everything about you now, James, but I will know, I'll know everything. Soon there'll be nothing about you that I don't know, and don't think that you'll ever be able to hide anything from me, because you won't be able to. You'll never be able to deceive me. Never.'

When her voice ceased, they looked at each other in amazement, then Jane said quietly, 'I don't know why I said that. I don't know where it came from.' She began to cry. James brought her a glass of water and as she drank he stroked her head.

'Are you angry?'

'No.'

'I'm really sorry.'

'That's all right.'

But when she looked up she saw that he was disturbed and frightened by what had happened. In silence they finished preparing for bed.

The following morning the woman who served them breakfast was as quiet as she could be, and the few remarks which she made were constructed so that no secondary meaning might be construed. It was of little consequence: Jane and James paid her no heed at all. They gazed at each other across the table with the apparent self-absorption of lovers. What they really felt was fear. They saw the gap that lay between them and were wondering already if it could ever be breached. When they looked at each other it was in blind terror, not blind love.

As they left the dining-room Jane said, 'It was a mistake ever to come here. Let's leave now. Let's go to the farm and start again: start properly.'

James agreed. They left the village later that day and drove to their home. And when James's father opened the door of the farm to them, Jane felt that she was looking into the future and seeing James as he would be in old age: seeing him as she would never see him in reality.

The shock of marriage did not diminish, but increased as Jane tried to settle into her new life and home. Like a Hindu woman she found herself in an arranged marriage, bound by passive acquiescence to a stranger: but it was she who had done the arranging. She had not, for example, given any significant thought to the fact that she and James would be sharing the farmhouse not only with her father-in-law, but also with the farm hand, Gerald. His presence rankled greatly with Jane, but James was quite implacable in the matter. It would have been foolish to have him lodge in some other farmhouse, he said, and it was also a more economical idea. They were able to give him a smaller wage because he had the spare room, and also was given his meals in the house. It meant, too, that if there was an emergency on the farm, he was on hand. If a cow got sick at night, or if a dog made its way in amongst the sheep, Gerald could deal with it. Jane did not see the logic of this, for when there was a crisis James invariably went to help Gerald, although it was rarely anything which one man could not have managed alone.

Jane felt ill at ease in the big house, which was draughty and uncomfortable. Mainly because of her father-in-law she could not put in motion the domestic changes which she desired: fresh wallpaper, new carpets, and brightly coloured paint. She sensed that James's father – and James too – liked the house to remain as it had always been. Her presence did nothing to change the womanless air of the place, and even she was struck by the oddness of it.

One day, not very long after their marriage, she came into the kitchen to find James cleaning out a large brown and black double-barrelled shot-gun.

'What's that for?' she asked falteringly.

'What do you think it's for?' he replied laughing. 'Killing things, that's what,' as he closed it with a click and playfully levelled the empty gun at her.

That night the weather was stormy, and the following morning James rose long before the dawn to go out wildfowling. When he had gone from the dim room Jane moved over to his side of the bed, into the warm depression which his body had made. Breathing in a smell of his absent body from the sheets and the soft pillow she listened, as she so often did, to the sound of the birds, but now their cries were broken by the sounds of the men's guns. She was surprised to find how much this upset her, for until then she had always associated the bird cries with hostility: often she had wished for a natural silence. She felt ill at ease in the countryside, for it was not 'nice' as she had vaguely imagined it would be, any more than marriage was 'nice'. The flat earth and the wide, wide sky frightened her, and to her the noise of the birds was the noise of nature: implacable, uncompromising, cruel: something which could not be contained or controlled. She was surprised, therefore, at the great pity which she felt for the birds as she lay in bed and thought of them, wounded and crying and frightened out there in the raw morning.

Later James came home, shamefaced at his lack of success. He threw a single mallard on the kitchen table, and Jane was shocked. She had never seriously thought of the birds as living creatures until that moment, when she saw one dead. She had considered them distant creatures and thought of them in terms of sound rather than of touch. At dusk she had watched them fly across the sky, pale against the turbid clouds: always something multiple, distant, untouchable. Never before had she been so close to a wild duck, and it filled her with wonder. For a long time she stood looking at the dead bird with a mixture of admiration and revulsion. Plump, solid and heavy-looking, its little dead eyes glittered, and its fabulous glossy feathers deflected the light. Forcing herself to put out her hand and stroke it, Jane thought gladly of all the other birds which were still out there, in the water and in the air: alive.

James's father plucked and cleaned out the bird and presented to Jane a lump of flesh that looked like nothing so much as a dismembered baby. It took the full power of her will to make her roast it in the oven. When it was ready she could not bear to watch the men eat the fowl, it make her sick even to think of it.

And then someone gave them a gift of fish and she had to cook that too, and then someone gave them a parcel of eels wrapped in thick black polythene which rolled and wriggled along the back step until James's father opened the package up and killed and skinned them. All this was a revelation to Jane: that you could live comfortably with nature to such a degree that it did not threaten you but that you threatened it: only when she realized this did Jane feel that she was beginning to understand this strange place where she was to spend the rest of her life.

Jane found it no easier to make friends in the country than she had in town: in fact, she soon found herself longing for the city's anonymity. At first she merely disliked going to the village to do shopping, but gradually the dislike grew to the point of dread. As she walked along the quiet main street she felt that someone peeped from every window. In shops she parried politely the sly, insinuating questions of the villagers, and always presented a face as blank as the fronts of the painted houses that watched her. Paranoia developed so that even when goodwill was shown to her she would not see it. She distrusted everyone, imagining a sneer in every greeting, and sarcasm in response to every remark she made. She felt that they hated her city accent and her different ways. The closed circle of the community would not open to admit her, and at last the day came when she flung her bags upon the kitchen table and said pettishly to James, 'You're to do the shopping from now on. I don't want to go back to the village again.' It took a good deal of questioning and coaxing before she would reveal what had finally made her so cross.

'I overheard two women talking,' she said at last. 'I'm sure that they were talking about me. They said that I was as odd as a pet hen.'

And when James laughed at this, she became angry and sulked for the rest of the day.

James had hoped that a strong friendship would develop between Jane and Ellen, the woman who lived in the cottage near by, but when they met for the first time it was with spontaneous and mutual antipathy, staring at each other with identical blue eyes.

The meeting took place at the cottage, and Ellen presided queen-like over a china teapot, with a gentility that made Jane hate her; and she hated her too for the prettiness of her small, dim cottage.

'I want to know all about you,' Ellen said. 'James has told me next to nothing.'

And so Jane began to tell the story of her life with her usual quiet confidence and secure belief in her powers of eloquence. But as she told her tale (which she could do now without giving much thought to either the matter or the method of the telling), she was unnerved to notice two things: first, that Ellen bore a distinct physical resemblance to herself; and second, that she obviously did not believe a word of what Jane was saying. The fire, the convent, the attic, the office: she thought that Jane was making it all up to solicit pity, and to give herself the spurious respectability of actually having had a past life. The combined effect of these two factors was that before she had finished speaking, Jane felt that she was listening to herself, and disbelieving the story of her own past life. She had never used this ploy for any other reason than to elicit sympathy, and never, until now, had it failed.

When she finished, Ellen picked up her teacup and before

taking a tiny sip threw two words into the silence, like small stones. 'How sad.'

'At least it has a happy ending,' said Jane. 'I was lucky to find James.'

'Yes, you were,' said Ellen flatly. There was an unpleasant pause.

'You must find it very lonely over here. Don't you find it lonely?'

'Not really – I have my job to do, and I have friends in the village. Gerald comes to see me sometimes. No,' said Ellen, 'I'm not lonely.' Jane said nothing. Ellen smiled sweetly at her and offered her more tea.

'We didn't get on,' Jane said flatly that night when James asked her how the visit had fared.

'Oh?' he said.

'No.'

'Why?'

'Why not?'

'That's no sort of an answer, Jane.' She shrugged her shoulders crossly.

'She didn't like me. I could feel it, and that made me dislike her. I don't know why it happened. You can't always know why you dislike another person, James, any more than you can always tell why you do like others.'

He did not reply, but it was obvious that he was disappointed by the outcome of the visit.

One curious result of the incident was that it brought Jane and her father-in-law much closer together, 'Stuck-up baggage,' he said. 'You're better off without her for a friend.'

Jane's antipathy towards Ellen was mixed with a considerable degree of curiosity, and she wanted to know all about her background. James would tell her nothing, but his father was happy to oblige. One winter's night as they sat by the stove, he told her the story of Ellen's past. Jane listened attentively and later she would run over it again and again in her mind, embellishing the tale with little added details of her own, imagining certain scenes with particular intensity. Every time she saw

Ellen thereafter, she would think of what she knew, conscious always that it was partly truth and partly her own invention.

Without ever knowing its history, Jane had frequently seen Ellen's birthplace. It stood on the outskirts of the village, and in its day had evidently been a fine house, with extensive lawns, tennis courts and a summer-house; elegantly furnished within and meticulously tended without. But its days of glory were long since over, for the house was now nothing more than a blackened, burnt-out shell. The neglected gardens grew wild, and where ladies had once played croquet, cattle now munched the grass and scratched their necks against the trunk of a sprawling white lilac.

Ellen had not been raised in luxury. The fall of the family had begun with her grandfather, who drank and gambled away a great deal of the family fortune. After his death his only son, Ellen's father, married and led a life of dissipation far surpassing that of his father's. Jane thought frequently of how greatly Ellen's mother must have been taken in by marriage. James's father spoke highly of the woman, and said, 'She made the most terrible mistake of her life in marrying that fool.' From the daughter, Jane was able to create in her mind a picture of the mother: frail, blue-eyed, refined. How utterly duped she must have been when first she saw the house! Jane imagined her coming to tea, intent on marriage and blinding herself to everything that might endanger the illusion in which she longed to believe. Later perhaps she would lie to herself, saying that it was dusk when they took tea in the drawing-room, and in the failing light she could see the maid's black and white uniform, but not the stains on her apron or how badly her cuffs were frayed; could see the Dresden china, but not the silverfish which flickered across the saucer when she raised her cup; could see the silver salvers on the dresser, but not the fact that they were yellow and tarnished. She knew in her heart that the dusk was a lie, for it had been an afternoon in summer: sunlight poured through the high windows. Ellen's mother saw then only the gentility she wanted to see: but when she came back to the house as a wife, she saw things very clearly indeed.

By force of necessity the small staff became smaller still: the grubby maid was dismissed, then the gardener, then the cook, until only the housekeeper remained. This woman did not live on the premises, and after her departure each evening, husband and wife would be left alone together in the huge, empty house. He drank heavily. Everything of value in the house (including the tarnished silver plate) was sold to meet increasing debts, and everything else began to decay. With a morbid interest, Jane tried to imagine how the woman must have felt at the creeping and inexorable decay of her home. She thought of her moving from one cold, empty room to another, watching as the big house rotted around her, and she could do nothing to stop it. Her reflection looked back at her from huge oval mirrors of bevelled glass, the mercury of which was stained brown. In the drawing-room, patches of damp spread across the parquet, and mildew crept up the velvet curtains. Books burst their spines in the damp library. Before her eyes, the painted faces of her husband's ancestors disintegrated and crumbled, just as their corporeal faces had long since rotted away in the family's ostentatious grave. One by one, the windows in the conservatory were broken until nothing remained but a frail cage of rotting white wood. After the birth of her daughter the woman must have wept to think of the harm the house might do to her child: no fires could defeat the damp, seeping cold; and in winter the rats would enter unchecked through the rotten floorboards and doors.

When Ellen was twelve, her father, overwhelmed by debts, took an ornamental revolver out to a ruined gazebo in the grounds of the house. His wife heard the report, and it was she who found her husband with half his head blown away. (The deed was, of course, in reality performed with a shotgun in the back yard: the revolver and gazebo were gothic fancies which Jane could not resist adding.) He was not buried in the family grave, but at the foot of the hill, in a patch of ground set aside for the bodies of suicides and unbaptized infants.

Jane's father-in-law said that all the villagers had presumed Ellen's mother would leave as soon as possible after the incident, but to everyone's astonishment, she made no move. She closed down most of the rooms of the big house, and lived with her daughter in one small wing. She no longer employed a housekeeper, but the woman who had filled that post remained her only friend in the village. The former housekeeper frequently visited the big house, and in return Ellen and her mother often visited the woman in her cottage. The bond between Ellen and the housekeeper was particularly strong; she filled for her the function of a grandmother, and often the child stayed overnight with her. It so happened that she was staying with the woman on the night fire broke out in the big house, and had she been at home, she would surely have died with her mother. The fire started in the wing to which they had confined themselves, but it spread rapidly, and by morning Ellen had no father, no mother, no home and no money. She was fifteen years old.

After the funeral, the housekeeper told Ellen that she was to come and live with her. The girl gladly did so, and continued her studies at the local school. The woman and the girl lived together happily, and when the woman died some years later, Ellen was as grieved as she had been by the death of her natural mother. She inherited the cottage, and was at that time just old enough to begin work, so she completed her studies in music and was fortunate enough to secure a teaching post at her old school in the nearby town. She continued to live quietly at the cottage.

'And are you sure that the fire was an accident?' said Jane.

'Of course it was,' her father-in-law replied. 'What would a fine woman like that want to kill herself for?'

'So then she's buried in the family grave?'

'No,' he said reluctantly. 'There was fools then that thought as you did – and bigger fools that thought she would want to be buried with that weak, drunken scut just because she had made the mistake of marrying him.'

'So she's at the foot of the hill too?' Jane said.

'Yes.'

'Odd that she did want to stay in the village after he died, wasn't it?'

'Yes,' said her father-in-law, but the telling of the tale had evidently wearied him, for he would say no more.

Jane's new life did not lose its sense of strangeness with the passage of time. She did not feel that she belonged in the big, cold farmhouse, and could not become used to the cruelty of nature, nor to the harshness of country life. Yet always there was a sense of distance which to some degree protected her, and she felt this in small matters as well as in more important things, so that when she opened the door one morning and found at her feet a disembowelled rat, left there by the farm cat, she could think, *This isn't really happening to me*. It was some other woman who had found herself living in a house where such things were commonplace, where there were slugs in the kitchen and enormous spiders in the bedrooms, and Jane was somehow able to observe this woman's plight with a peculiar intimacy.

But it was Jane who failed to know and be known by her husband. She knew then that the sense of distance did not protect her, but was instead what was so fundamentally wrong with her life. As the weeks and months went by, she did not feel that she was becoming any closer to him, and she did not know how to go about creating that closeness. It almost drove her mad with anger to think that Ellen, by the simple fact of having lived near by for many years, probably knew him better than she did. They had so little time together. All day, both of them would be working, and in the evenings Gerald sometimes went across the fields to visit Ellen, while James's father would go to the village pub for a few hours, but their socializing rarely seemed to coincide, and one or other of the two men always seemed to be around when Jane least wanted company. Even when she and James were alone in a room, there was always the possibility that someone would come in unexpectedly. The only real privacy they had was when they were in their bedroom, but Jane was dismayed to find that the longer they lived together, the more uncomfortable they were in each other's company. In time, she almost began to dread being with him, for the combination of affection and distance in which they lived upset her. It dismayed her to discover time and time again that there were so many things which she could not do. She could not bring herself to be open with him and honest; could not overcome the fear which she had of cultivating intimacy. It made her tell lies: one day when James unexpectedly asked her if she was happy she replied, 'Yes, of course.' They did not understand each other. The physical side of their marriage was unsatisfactory too, for although the house was old, the interior walls were thin, and the thought that either Gerald or James's father might overhear their love-making embarrassed and inhibited them both. After many months together she wanted to say to him, 'Is this it? Is this how it will always be?' But she did not ask, because she was afraid of how he would answer.

And then, a year to the day since her marriage, her aunt turned up, uninvited and unannounced, wanting to see what her niece had made of her life.

'You never told me just how much of a wilderness you live in,' were her aunt's first words. 'The nearest life miles away, and that no more than a clutch of half-witted yokels, the most of them cross-eyed with inbreeding.' Jane was inclined to agree with this, but she remained in sullen silence. She agreed with a surprising amount of what her aunt said in the course of her three-hour visit: they were things which Jane had thought to herself time without number in the course of the year, but she was outraged to hear her aunt articulate these damning judgements of Jane's life. She sneered at Jane for the rough aspect of the house: cigarette burns on the clothless kitchen table; tattered cushions, dowdy curtains, and a few hens picking around the back door.

'It suits us,' Jane shrugged.

'Marriage. A funny kind of marriage, if you ask me, with three husbands to cook and care for.'

'I enjoy it,' she lied.

'Three husbands and no children. Any on the way?'

'No!' Jane snapped.

Now it was her aunt's turn to shrug. 'Funny kind of marriage,' she said again.

'It's none of your concern.' Jane struggled to find the right words. 'And I'm very happy here with James.'

'Say that often enough and you might begin to believe it,' her aunt replied. 'Say it too often, and people will know for sure that you don't.'

Late that evening, James found Jane leaning on the gate at the bottom of the yard, apparently just looking out across a field of barley, but when he spoke to her and she turned around, he saw that she was crying. She cried for the rest of that night, and for most of the next day. James thought that it was due merely to her aunt's visit, and that the woman's presence had reminded Jane of a part of her life which she very much wanted to forget; and Jane let him think this, even though it was not the true matter of the case. For when her aunt spoke of children, she had forced into speech a topic about which Jane had not even allowed herself to think. Now she could think of little else, and soon persuaded herself that the lack of children was not just another of her troubles, but the principal cause.

If they had a baby, things would be better. Then they would have a real marriage, and not this parody of a family in which she now lived with, as her aunt had so neatly, cruelly put it, three husbands and no children. If she were to become a mother, she thought, she would have more power in the farm. She would be able to lay for ever the ghost of James's mother, whose presence she still felt too strongly in the house, and which she could not accept. (At night Jane always sat by the kitchen stove: nothing would have induced her to relax in that mausoleum of a parlour.) If she became a mother, then she was bound to be more than just the keeper of the house. Then things would have to change.

The farm had four bedrooms: one was shared by Jane and James, one was for James's father, one for Gerald, and the fourth lay empty. It was to this last room that Jane now began to go at odd moments of the day, for it was this room, more than any other in the house, which she now wanted to change. In her mind, she had designated it as a future nursery, and would sit there in the dusty silence, while sunlight fell on faded wall-paper, thinking of how it would look when refurbished. There would be curtains with rabbits on them, soft rugs and a white cradle; instead of this dreary wallpaper, the high, wide bed, and the cupboard like a confessional.

But nothing happened. Once more she was finding that there were matters in which the strength of her will was useless. Her body continued to fail her, month after month. She could not bring herself to speak to James about it, but before long suspected that he knew what was troubling her. When his father one day, speaking of the farm, said lightly, 'I wonder if there'll be another generation to work the land when we're not here,' the temper and embarrassment with which James responded confirmed her suspicions. From then on, the problem was acknowledged between them, but still without words. James became short with his father and with Gerald, but increasingly protective and defensive about Jane. They made love more frequently, but it became a mechanical procedure, and by this time Jane hated her body so much that she wanted no pleasure from it. She saw it as a thing apart from her, a thing that was failing her and she wanted to punish it.

But she never lost hope completely. Every time they made love she could tell herself afterwards that perhaps the problem was over, perhaps she was already pregnant and it would only be a matter of time before she knew it. But she grew to put too much store by that 'perhaps', and every time another month passed, her grief on discovering that she was still not pregnant was easily matched by her astonishment.

James found her one afternoon crying on the bed of the spare room.

'You ought to go to the doctor, Jane,' he said awkwardly.

'Why just me?' she said at once, 'It might be your fault.' And as soon as the words were out she knew that they would not go, and she knew why. She could hear the doctors putting the blame on one or other of them. Although the uncertainty in which they now lived was a torment to her, still she knew that it was preferable to the scientific certainty which the doctors might provide. Her hope was slender, and foolish, but it was there, and she was not ready to risk losing it.

'I'm sorry,' she said. 'I don't want to go to the doctor's – not yet a while, anyway.'

They were well into the second year of their marriage by this time. Gerald was still a frequent visitor to Ellen in the cottage, but Jane paid little heed to the pair, as she was too preoccupied with her own problems. She did not appear to be particularly interested when James came into the scullery one day and said, 'I've just been talking with Gerald. He says that himself and Ellen are getting married.'

'Bully for them,' said Jane flatly. James frowned.

'Ellen says that you can be her matron of honour, if you like.'

Jane smiled at the way in which the offer was phrased. 'I don't think that I'd be worthy of that.'

'Gerald asked me to be his best man. I said yes, of course.'

Jane did not reply.

Because of the manner in which she received the news, James was astonished when Jane said casually a few days later, 'I went over to see Ellen today, to congratulate her on her marriage. I asked her if she'd like to borrow my wedding dress.'

'That was very kind of you,' said James. Jane shrugged.

'She was surprised, I think, but she said that she'd consider the offer. It *is* a very nice dress.'

The couple were to be married in the early summer. The weather became warm and then hot – unnaturally hot for the time of year. Jane noticed that James was becoming increasingly moody and tense, and that he was finding it more difficult all the time to conceal these feelings. Then, one day in June, she was standing by the door of the house looking out across the flat land with James by her side. Before them was a big tree, and it was full of starlings: twittering and screeching, they made the whole tree seem alive with the weight and the noise of them. James suddenly pushed past her into the house, and emerged a moment later with his shot-gun. He fumbled as he slotted two cartridges into it, then snapped it shut, aimed and fired twice. Jane's ears boomed with the noise of the gun's report, and as she watched the birds went up in a cloud of black, screeching in terror. After a few moments she went over to the rutted path where some of the birds had fallen. James ambled after her, the gun now broken across his arm. She was afraid to count the birds that were dead, there were so many of them. One bird was still alive. Its speckled feathers were clotted with blood, and it opened its beak again and again as if trying to cry, but no noise came. James saw it. He walked over to the bird, and put his foot upon its breast. He steadily pressed it down into the rutted mud, pressed harder and harder until blood spurted from the bird's silent, gaping beak. Jane felt that she ought to look away, but could not bring herself to do so: she watched unblinkingly while her husband crushed the starling under his foot. When it was done, he turned and walked back to the house without speaking a word.

Four days later, Ellen and Gerald were married. The coolness of the little village chapel should have been a respite from the heat of the day, but Jane felt a suffocating warmth as she sat by her father-in-law, waiting for the ceremony to begin. Looking around her she saw the coloured figures of mild saints burn in stained glass, and above the pew where she was sitting there was a window depicting the baptism of Jesus in the river Jordan. A bee had flown into the church, and was trapped at this window, striving for the light. Jane watched it obsessively, vainly, and she felt for it as it battered its little woolly body against the glass and nervously buzzed. Then the church organ groaned into life: the wedding party had arrived.

For Jane, the ceremony was a nightmare. Ellen had accepted the offer of the wedding dress, and the gesture now backfired against Jane, for she felt that she was watching herself being married, and married to the wrong man. As she stared at Ellen's narrow white back, this feeling grew so intense that she could feel stiff white lace around her wrists, and she could see the altar close to and through a veil. Jane breathed in deeply, heard the bee buzz and her father-in-law cough beside her; closed her eyes, opened them, and again Gerald was kneeling by her side. Helpless, she watched the wedding progress. James produced from his pocket a golden ring, while his wife's soul floated back and forth through the tiny chapel, from the prie-dieu in the sanctuary, to the hard pew beneath the coloured window, where the anxious bee was still trapped.

At the wedding breakfast, James in his role of best man was obliged to sit at the top table, and so Jane again sat beside her father-in-law. Neither of them was happy: Jane felt shy and ill at ease amongst the crowds of boisterous wedding guests; her father-in-law was discontented about everything. He complained frequently about the heat, and squirmed miserably in his good suit and stiff shirt and tie. While the speeches droned on they caught each other's eye and smiled sadly; and when the music began, it was more than they could bear. Together they slipped out of the room, and went out into the gardens of the hotel where the wedding breakfast was being held. They linked arms and walked for a short distance, then sat down upon a bench beneath some trees. The old man loosened his tie and undid the top buttons of his shirt. Then he said something completely unexpected.

'She had a great notion of James, once.'

'Who had?'

'Who do you think? Ellen, of course.'

'Ellen?'

'Aye, Ellen. She'd have married him too, if she could have managed it.'

Jane did not reply. She was too amazed. Never had she imagined such a thing, but she did not feel angry or jealous. She felt elated. James had chosen her, and not Ellen. In her marriage, Ellen was resigning herself to a husband who was second choice, second best.

'When was this?' she asked curiously.

Neither Jane nor her father-in-law realized that at that moment James was watching them from a window of the hotel. He was surprised to see his wife and his father under the trees, so deep in conversation; but before he could think much about it, someone came up to speak to him, and led him back into the centre of the room, where his presence was requested. James did not see, therefore, that the conversation in the garden continued for a very long time. It would have been apparent, even from the distant window, that they were speaking with increasing intensity; that the old man was becoming upset, and that Jane was attempting to soothe him. Eventually she stood up, stood with her hand on his shoulder for quite some time, then turned and walked away through the grounds of the hotel.

The heat of the day and the strain of the occasion had given her a headache. Jane found another shaded bench, far distant from the one on which she had previously been sitting, and she stayed there for a long time, hoping that the pain would go away. Instead, it grew even worse, and at last she decided to go back into the hotel, where perhaps someone would have tablets: at least she would get a drink of cold water. She wanted to avoid seeing her father-in-law again, but the grounds were deceptively small, and when she rounded the corner of the building, she saw him on the other end of the gravel path on which she was standing. He was bent over a flower bush as though admiring the blossoms, and she was wondering if she would be able to slip past unnoticed when she saw him sway. Before she could reach him, he fell to the ground. He was speechless with pain.

'I'll go and get help,' she said, but he caught hold of her hand and would not release her from his tight grip.

Ellen and Gerald were leaving on their honeymoon. In the distance was the sound of voices and laughing as the wedding party came out on to the steps. Jane cried aloud for help, but no one heard her and no one came.

A few moments later, James came around the side of the hotel. He was puzzled and annoyed by the absence of his father and his wife. People had been asking where they were. He thought that they could have made a greater effort to participate. As he walked through the garden looking for them, he was prepared to be angry. He was not prepared for what he found: Jane kneeling at the end of a gravel path, with his father, dead, cradled in her arms.

A day later, his body was brought home to be waked. They laid him out in the room which Jane had designated the nursery.

Because of the hot weather they kept open the windows of the room: from the garden the smell of stocks drifted up at dusk. Once, when Jane went into the room, she found James there alone, looking at his father.

'He told me once that when I was born – here in this very room – he was waiting outside. The midwife came out and she was carrying a basin. It was full of blood. She told him to take it downstairs and pour it into the drain, then bring the basin back up to the room again. He told me that when she was lying dead in this same room.'

Those days were like a dream. The people who had been to the wedding now came back, sombre and in dark clothes. The priest who had solemnized the marriage now said the prayers for the dead. It seemed to Jane that every room in her house was now full of strangers. There was an unending round of tea and sandwiches and little buns. Sleepless for two nights, Jane found herself wishing that all this would end: that all these people would go home and that Gerald and her father-in-law would come back and let the house slide into its normal routine – and then she realized that that life had gone as absolutely as her life in the convent.

And then, suddenly, it was all over, and they were alone. In the evening they made a meal and then, exhausted, Jane and James went upstairs. They undressed and went to bed, curled up in each other's arms like weary children, and immediately they fell into a deep and dreamless sleep. They were so tired that they did not even close the door of the room or draw the curtains, so that when they awoke the following morning all the silence of the house, and all the emptiness of the rooms flooded up to their door. She could hear the muffled beat of the grandfather clock in the hall. It had measured out every moment of those last difficult years, and now she felt that she had awoken not only from the nightmare of the preceding two days, but of those two years. She felt as if they might as well have lasted for no more than two beats of the clock, and to measure all that past suffering in terms of time was meaningless. She lay back and let the emptiness of the house wash over her, while the dawn light streamed through the high, uncurtained windows, and fell upon the bed. Now they could begin. For the first time, the noise of the birds did not sound alien, but natural as music. She burrowed up against James until he too awoke. They looked at each other rather solemnly, and they did not speak. He touched her face and then her hair, which lay webbed out across the pillow, touched her gently, as if she were a new creature who had appeared by his side during the night, and whose reality he had to prove. And then she began to touch his body and to kiss him, her mouth opening softly and her tongue gently probing into his mouth; her hair falling like a dark veil across his face. They made love in the empty, sunlit house with more abandon and more tenderness than ever before in all their married life, and afterwards they lay in each other's arms, silent and naked, while the wild birds still cried out over the water.

CHAPTER FOUR

Peter walks into the room and sits down. Before him on the desk is a large Perspex block, like an outsize paperweight of the type that usually contains dried grasses, or tiny seashells. This one, contains a dead rat: supine and with its belly split open, its skin peeled elegantly back, and its veins and arteries stained a violent shade of blue and red. All its parts are neatly labelled. Shuddering, Peter quickly puts a book on top of it, and pushes it to one side. He looks up at the children before him, and against his will his glance wanders past them and around the room, which contains many other distressing sights: a gaudy wall-chart depicting a dissected eyeball; a shelf bearing the skulls of some small mammals; a little tank in which resides a small, glum toad. Peter nervously glances back at the children. They stare at him unblinking, and he tells them to sit down. The absent biology teacher has left work for them to do, so they take out their books, open them, and begin. It is three o'clock on a Friday afternoon, and the children fidget frequently: they are bored with work, and are eagerly anticipating the weekend. Peter sympathizes with them, for he shares their feelings, but he hopes that they will be able to contain themselves for the next hour, and allow him to maintain order. He too opens a book, but he only pretends to read, as many of the children before him only pretend to study.

Sitting directly in front of him is a girl named Katie. Discreetly, he leans forward to see what she is drawing in her book, and feels faintly revolted when he realizes that she is laboriously copying out of her textbook a diagram representing the human embryo. He likes Katie. She is idle, stupid, good-natured, and he prefers her to the diligent, intelligent and sly girls whom he has to teach. The older the classes are, the less comfortable he feels in their presence, and he is truly afraid of the sixth formers.

Katie lifts her head, and in reaching for ruler and rubber notices that her teacher is watching her. Peter is quite taken aback by the wide, suggestive grin which she gives him. He continues to watch her. A brace of thin, cheap bangles (the school rules forbid all jewellery) tinkles seductively along Katie's plump forearm as she neatly labels the diagram, and then begins to write notes on the facing page in her sprawling, childish handwriting. Peter looks down upon the crown of her head: her thick blonde hair is held back from her face by two absurd little clips with plastic flowers attached to them. Peter is about to smile, when suddenly he remembers another fair head adorned in just such a childish fashion. The face of the girl concerned is buried in a pillow and she is weeping so loudly that Peter thinks in alarm that he has, in his ignorance, perhaps done her a serious physical injury. He moves to stroke the shuddering head, but she pushes him away and cries even more bitterly. Remembering this, Peter does not smile, but winces.

Peter has other memories of things which he would prefer to forget. Another fair-haired girl watches him as he prepares to leave her room. She watches without any display of feeling or emotion, and he cannot help but imagine the contempt and disgust she must feel. He crosses the shabby room until he is standing close by her, and he looks down at her face, at the bleached hair, the hard mouth and the tired eyes.

'I suppose that you hate men very much,' he says.

The fair-haired girl's face still shows no feeling as she replies, 'No more than you hate women.'

Peter is fool enough to be shocked by this, and even more of a fool to protest, but the girl interrupts him. 'Next time you see a little boy playing in the street with a toy gun, watch him carefully. Watch him until a woman comes along. Watch him wait until she has passed him by a safe distance, and then, watch his glee when he shoots her in the back.'

Abruptly she turns aside and she yawns, passing her hand across her mouth with a certain lazy little gesture which Peter has seen an infinite number of times before this, for when Peter's mother yawns, she too puts her hand to her mouth in exactly the same way, her fingers at just such an angle for precisely the same few seconds. To see this woman make this gesture sends a tremor of shock through Peter: for a moment, he can almost believe that she *is* his mother, and that he is the child who will never escape, who will be watched forever, no matter how shameful or intimate the moment. In his anger, he moves to strike the yawning girl, but she flinches away and he misses. For a few moments there is silence, and then, for the first time that evening, a show of genuine feeling comes across the girl's face: she smiles. Then she gestures towards the door, silently bidding him to go.

Yes: his way of seeing women dates from that particular night. How easy, he thinks, it had been until then, for looking at his mother he simply saw his mother, and looking at any other woman he simply saw a stranger's face. But since that night, the barrier dividing his mother from all other women has been broken for ever. On going home, he might see in her loved and disappointed face the look of a girl he has tried to seduce a few nights earlier, and whom he thought he had already forgotten; and in the face of another such girl the following week, he might suddenly see through to such loneliness that he can think only of his mother, lying wakeful and alone in the cottage bedroom, as she has lain alone, night after night, for twenty years. He sees his mother's life as a wheel, turning around him, the graceless, ungrateful hub. He remembers the real panic which he felt as he entered his final year at training college, knowing that soon he will have to make a conscious choice about what he will do on leaving. But what alternative is there to going home? He has no great desire to stay in the city, for his life there is empty. He has a few male friends and with women he feels ill at ease, believing that there ought always to be a sexual dimension. Yet every time he goes back to the cottage his mother's love greets him like a furnace, belies the love of any other woman for Peter or of Peter for them; and he goes back to the city more wounded and empty than ever before.

But then, in the early spring of that final year, he begins a relationship with a girl which does not end quickly, like so many others, but continues on. Peter pleads excessive work as his exams approach, and does not go home for the weekends, but soon he is telling himself that even if he did go back, the relationship is strong enough to withstand the force of his mother's love. For the first time ever, he believes himself to be happy. The affair is an end in itself, and they drift on thoughtlessly, until the day comes when the girl tells him that she thinks she may be pregnant.

Nothing could have prepared Peter for the shock of this: no, not shock: sheer horror. For two days he walks around dazed and almost physically sick. His supposed love for the girl of course dies at once, like a candle in a high wind, and he wonders what his mother will say.

He phones her that night, perversely and against his better judgement, and he wants to weep when he hears the softness that comes into her voice as soon as she realizes that she is speaking to her son.

'Peter!' No one else has ever spoken his name with such sincere tenderness, and he feels guilty to think that he can give her such enormous pleasure simply by phoning her. Almost at once she asks, 'Is there anything wrong, Peter?'

'No,' he replies nervously, 'why should there be?'

'You sound a little worried.'

'My exams begin in three weeks,' he says, which is a true statement, but not an honest response to her implied question. She tells him not to overwork, and he promises moderation.

But Peter in turn can tell by her voice that she is excited about something, and she hesitates to say what it is, until the very moment when he is about to hang up. Then she interrupts him, and says very quickly that the post of English teacher has been advertised for the local school, to begin in the autumn. She adds nothing further, and Peter says 'Oh.'

She does not reply. In the silence from her end of the phone he can sense her loneliness and tension, and he breathes deeply.

'Well, be sure and get me an application form,' he says.

'I have one here,' she replies. 'I'll post it in the morning.'

Thereafter, Peter dumbly follows fate. The girl comes back and tells him that the pregnancy was a false alarm. The affair is concluded but only after a most bitter row, in which the girl says many cruel and perceptive things which wound Peter deeply. The form arrives and he fills it in; he works for his exams; sits them; passes them. He is appointed to the post in the local school. Privately and indefinitely he renounces women; then packs his bags, leaves the city and goes home to his mother.

Peter hears a snigger: a loud snigger. He realizes that it must have been growing as a groundswell for some time now, but he has been too immersed in his own thoughts to notice it. He silences them now with an anger which startles even him, and he is annoyed to feel his face go warm and red. Peter has been teaching for just over six months, but already he feels that he has never known any other reality but this little world of ink and chalk and books and desks and power and bells and children.

Rising from his desk, Peter walks across the room, and he does not take a book with him, not even for the pretence of work. He stops by the window and stands for a long time with his back to the class, and he looks out over the playing fields. A cold winter dusk thickens the air, and some drops of rain spit against the glass. The window-sill is cluttered with an array of dusty fossils and shells, out of which Peter carefully selects one: a little grey ammonite. It lies in the heart of his cupped hand like an egg in a nest, and gradually he feels the coldness of the dead stone take on the warmth of his small, live hand. How he detests his dainty little hands! Ridiculously out of proportion to the rest of his body, they look like the hands of a young girl. Now, however, as he gazes into his palm, Peter finds himself forgetting the rest of his body to the point where it no longer seems to exist; all his life has gone into this feminine hand, for which he now feels a new empathy, an acceptance, never before known. And in that moment, the physical knowledge of what it is to be a woman goes through him and is gone. He is left standing hurt and bewildered, knowing that this has happened only seconds before, yet already he has forgotten it.

The little grey fossil is lying still in his palm, and now he thinks of Sarah lying full length upon the parlour sofa in the cottage. It is the last Saturday before Christmas, and she is holding in her hand the smooth, speckled sea shell which he has just given to her.

How strange and unexpected all this business with Sarah has been! He has always taken her for granted. Throughout his life, she had been a very infrequent friend. Of all the family at the farm, she is the only one who has ever found the company of his mother and himself at least tolerable, let alone agreeable. At times he wonders if she visits him just to be perverse, to annoy her mother, and, more lately, Catherine. The difference that there can be between sisters! And twin sisters at that! The fondness he has always had for Sarah is offset by his deep dislike of Catherine, a dislike which has grown in recent years into contempt.

At least I made an attempt, he thinks, remembering a day the preceding summer, when he took the rowing boat out on the lough. Catherine, out for a walk, had chanced along, and he had felt obliged to ask her if she wanted to go out too. She did go: perhaps out of politeness, and she spoke to him with a shy formality until they had been on the water for about twenty minutes, when suddenly she would speak no more. She scrambled out hastily when they reached the shore again, did not offer to help him beach the boat, did not thank him or say goodbye, but quickly walked away across the fields, heading for the farmhouse. Since then, Peter has paid no heed to her, and himself barely deigns to speak when they meet. Strange that she did not go off to the convent after all, when that was what she had wanted so much. Place for her too, Peter bitterly thinks, closed away for the rest of her life. Might as well be dead as live like that, and damn the loss she'd be to the world. But Sarah will not speak of the matter. He sees her again standing at the cottage door on a day in autumn, when her visits had again become frequent and regular. Incidentally, almost, she says as she leaves:

'By the way, my sister won't be going into the convent after all.'

'Oh?'

'No.'

'Why did she change her mind? She was so set on it . . .'

But Sarah interrupts him, frowning slightly and she says, 'I didn't say that she changed her mind. I just said that she won't be going away.' She frowns more deeply, and she leaves the cottage, the subject never to be mentioned again.

Since his return from training college at the start of the preceding summer, Sarah has been a frequent visitor, coming first on the occasional Saturday, when Peter's mother was away giving music lessons, but by early autumn she had begun to call every week without fail. In retrospect, he thinks that Sarah also changed slightly around that time. She was quieter and more abstracted (although often more irritable too), and her conversation was somehow more impersonal and inconsequential than it had been until then. But it is only a month or so now since things really began to change. Peter goes back in his mind to that particular mid-December day. The weather is bitterly cold, and Sarah is gathering holly. From the cottage window he watches her pull down branches from the tall hedge, and then load them into a little wheelbarrow which she has brought with her. Her task complete, she pushes the barrow to the cottage door, and Peter lets her in. For a while they sit talking by the parlour fire, and he sees that her hands are cold and hurt, livid and scratched by the holly. He leaves her there to continue warming herself, while he goes into the kitchen to make tea. He puts the kettle on the hob, and while he waits for it to boil he remains in the kitchen, looking idly out of the window.

The whole weight of his body is leaning upon his hands, which rest upon the edge of the work surface, when suddenly a red, scratched hand comes to rest very hesitantly and gently upon one of his rather small hands. Startled, for he did not hear her walk softly from the parlour, he turns around and immediately she puts her arms around him, still very gentle and hesitant, as if she expects him to pull away in shock or disgust at any moment. He does not reject her: but he is shocked. He has not been touched by a woman for months. She does little more than stand there and embrace him, but she does lean her head against his shoulder, and he is further transfixed. He cannot tell how long they have been standing there before it occurs to him to put his arms around her, and he does this, awkwardly. She looks up then, and she smiles at him. He smiles back.

By now the kettle has begun to screech, and the kitchen is filled with steam. The cold window is all misted over, and she releases him so that he can lower the gas and attend to the tea while she returns silently to the parlour. But when he walks in a few moments later carrying the tray, the room is empty. Her boots have gone from the hallway, and when he looks out of the cottage window, he can see that she is well on her way home, pushing the laden barrow before her.

When his mother returns that evening, Peter is so quiet that she thinks something is wrong, and asks him what has happened.

'Nothing,' he replies, 'nothing at all.' And technically it is no lie, for next to nothing has happened. The afternoon's incident was probably the most tentative and inconsequential physical encounter that he has ever had with a woman, but its potential significance far outweighs the event itself. Perhaps she has been quiet and strange for these past few weeks because she has been working round to this: or perhaps she acted purely on impulse, because she was lonely and he was the only man available. Maybe at this very moment she was regretting what she had done, and would be too embarrassed to come to the cottage again. Or perhaps she would return and try to pretend that nothing at all had happened. He certainly never imagined that such a thing might develop. By that night, he has decided that he will let matters take their own course. It is up to Sarah now: it was she, after all, who made the first move.

During the succeeding week, he thinks about the incident less and less, and by Saturday has persuaded himself that she will not come to the cottage again.

But she does return, and she puts her arms around him again. She continues to visit the cottage every Saturday, so that by the new year a pattern has been well established. Peter knows that he is quite passive in this whole affair, and that Sarah alone directs the relationship and sets its pace. They do just what she wants, and talk only on the limited topics of her choice. Yet so skilfully does she manipulate the situation that at times Peter feels she can control his will indirectly; as though without her telling him he knows what she wants him to do, and he dumbly complies. He sees suddenly that he has no dignity in this matter, and that this lack of dignity is all his own fault.

Peter feels that the whole thing could stop again as quickly as it started. He does not know why Sarah has made the friendship take this particular direction, any more than he did on that first day, when she gathered the holly. Once, she actually stopped at the door and said, 'Peter, I want to tell you . . .' But then there was a long pause, broken only when she hit the door jamb hard with her fist and said, 'Nothing.'

Again he sees her lying on the sofa, holding that shell, and in his memory, Sarah says, 'If only pain were like a shell or a stone. We could pick it up, but we could put it down too, we could cast it away. The hardest things are always the things you can't touch or smell or see or hear. You begin to wonder then if this terrible thing is perhaps just imaginary.'

She is quiet for some time, then thanks him again for the gift. He has no inkling of the nature of the pain she wishes to make tangible. Until then, he had not realized that she was so very unhappy.

He glances up, and sees that the children have discreetly begun to tidy away their books in anticipation of the bell. Peter replaces the fossil on the sill, and in the relief he feels at his hand's sudden emptiness thinks how right Sarah was. If only all his loneliness and discontent could be instilled into a little thing which could be set down quietly on a shelf and abandoned for ever. But when he crosses the room, back to his position of authority at the teacher's desk, all his worries go with him. Waiting for the bell, he realizes that he is every bit as anxious for it to ring as the children are, for it marks the start of the weekend. Tomorrow is Saturday, and Sarah will come to him.

The clock hand moves to the quarter hour, and the electric bell rings throughout the school with a loud, steely sound. The children explode out of the biology lab, and as Peter gathers together his own books, he sees that only one child remains. Fair-haired Katie gives him a sweet smile as she lingeringly replaces all her coloured pencils, one by one and side by side, in their flat tin box.

CHAPTER FIVE

On the morning after the funeral, James rose first from the bed, and as Jane lay there watching him dress, she hoped that in the coming days she would be able to hide the relief which she now felt. Jane was grateful for the quietness and privacy afforded in the house by the death of her husband's father, and knew that James would be hurt to think that she greeted the death so gladly. She thought tenderly of how she would ease her husband through his loss.

Jane was astonished, therefore, when later that day she found the old man's tobacco pouch and pipe under a cushion where he had tucked them away: when she took them in her hands she began to cry uncontrollably, so that it was James who had to comfort her. The early elation passed very quickly, and Jane felt a deep sense of loss. She had not realized how much she depended upon his company while she did household tasks around the kitchen, and James and Gerald were out working in the fields, had not realized until now, when it was too late and he was gone.

But she felt anger too, for she envied James his father's death as much as she had envied him his life. He had had the comfort of living with his parents for over twenty years, and now he had had the further comfort of their deaths and burials.

'Being Jane' had always meant being on more than nodding terms with death: it had meant being familiar with it in a very particular way. All her life she had defined herself in terms of death, because she was the child of dead parents (and that had always seemed to hold the possibility of their being no parents at all). Reluctantly now, she had to admit that her knowledge of death was knowledge by default. She knew it only by its absence, while James knew it more intimately by its occasional intrusion into his life. His mother had died there in the farmhouse when he was twenty. It was James who shot the wildfowl and gutted fish: Jane could not have killed an animal to save her own life. James often went to wakes around the countryside, and was familiar with the sight of dead people, but before the death of her father-in-law, Jane had never seen a dead person. Death had not been a presence, then, but a lack: lack of family, lack of love, lack of a real home. This had made her feel particularly conscious of life itself, and of how terrible it was always to have to live in that state of lack and need.

It was difficult to break away from old habits: despite the fact that they now had the whole house to themselves, they still only felt truly at ease in their bedroom, and could never bring themselves to speak of James's father in any other place. They felt as though it would be a violation to talk of the man's death in the rooms which they had once shared with him. And Jane dreaded the way that her husband went back to the subject time and time again.

One night when they were lying in bed in the darkness he whispered to her, 'Tell me about it. Tell me how he died.'

'I've told you before, James. There's not really a lot to tell.'

'What were his last words?'

'I don't remember,' she said, but she said it too quickly. James had been stroking her shoulder, and stopped when she said this. He knew that she was lying.

'Perhaps he said "Help me",' she said. 'He was in pain. It was some little thing he was saying, I don't remember the last words exactly, James. I'm sorry.' He started to stroke her shoulder again, and there was a silence so long that she was beginning to think with relief that the matter was ended for another night, when he said, 'Tell me exactly what happened, Jane.'

'I've told you before, James,' she said wearily.

'Again. Please, Jane. I know it's hard for you to go over it all again, but please – for me.'

'When the music started,' she said very slowly and evenly, moving closer to him as she spoke, 'we went out into the grounds of the hotel. We walked for a little time, and then sat down. We talked. We talked for some time, and then he said that he would sit there and rest because he was very tired. I was still stiff from sitting all through the wedding and the meal, so I went for a walk – just a short walk, and when I came back, he was bent over a flower bush. When I went up to him he collapsed. As I say, I think he may have said something like "Help me", but I can't say for sure. He held on to me very tightly when I put my arms around him, and he died very quickly. He died just the moment before you found us.'

They were both silent for a long time, and again she hoped that he was placated, when again he spoke, softly and persistently.

'And before you left him?'

'Yes?'

'You were talking?'

'Yes.'

'What were you talking about, Jane?'

Jane wanted to wail, 'I promised that I wouldn't tell!' but she knew that this would open up a breach between them that would last for the rest of their lives. Of course James's suspicions were correct. She moved even closer to him, grateful for the blackness.

'James, I know what you're thinking about, and you're right,' she lied. 'When I went into the garden with your father, he had had a bit too much to drink. Because it was Ellen's wedding, we were talking about Ellen. He told me that she had once had a great notion of you, that she even wanted to marry you, but that you would have none of it.' James did not speak. 'Isn't that what you're thinking about?'

'Yes.' She let him stay silent, and at last he said, 'I didn't tell you, because it didn't seem important at first. It was just one of those things. Often people have all sorts of things in their past, and it's foolish to think that just because you marry a person or because you love them, that you have to tell them about those things, when they're long over and gone. That would be foolish, wouldn't it, Jane?'

'Yes,' she replied, and she could hardly get the little word out for anger and jealousy; wanted to wring from him any other little secrets which he might happen to be hiding.

'I was going to tell you about Ellen because she lived so near, and then I didn't because I thought that you might be hurt. I was afraid on both counts, for I was afraid that you might hear gossip that would make it sound worse than ever it was; and I thought that if I didn't tell you then perhaps no one would. Daddy had promised me that he would say nothing, so in the end I decided to leave well alone. Particularly after you met Ellen and didn't take to her. It seemed cruel and pointless to annoy you with something that's finished and gone. Are you angry with me now because I didn't tell you?'

'No,' she said, 'no, of course not.' It was true: any jealousy she felt was killed by the relief of knowing that he would never again pester her to know what his father had told her on the day of the wedding.

James was moved by her generous forgiveness. 'I'm glad that you were with him when he died,' he said. 'He was very fond of you, you know. He couldn't have loved you more, not if you had been his own daughter.'

'I was very fond of him too,' she said, 'but when I die, I want to die alone.'

'Jane!'

'I do. I don't want anyone to watch me dying. Will you promise me that, James? That is if the circumstances are such that you can, that you'll leave me in peace?'

'This is foolish. You're being morbid.'

'I'm not being morbid, or silly, I'm quite serious. Promise me.'

'I don't know that I want to.'

'Well, you have to. Promise, no, swear, that when I'm dying that you won't stay and watch me, but that you'll leave me to die alone.'

'Very well then,' he said. 'I promise.'

'Swear it, James.'

'All right then, silly – and you are silly, and morbid too. I promise and I swear, and there's an end to it.'

About a week after this incident, Jane began the process of

clearing out and taking over the house to make of it the home she wanted. She began in the room which she hated most of all – the parlour – and she began surreptitiously, so that it would not upset James too much. While making plans in her mind, she rummaged through cupboards and drawers, some of which she had never even opened since coming to the house. On the first day of her task, she found at the back of a musty press a little cloth bag which, when she tipped it out on to the kitchen table, she found to contain about a score of sea shells. After careful thought, she left them there as a wordless suggestion to James of the process which she had set in motion. And when James did come in a few hours later he was on the point of speaking, but on seeing the shells he did not speak. Instead, he sat down at the table, and for a long time he simply looked at them, piled there in disorder, looked at them in silence. When at last he did stretch out his hand to touch them, he did so with hesitancy and restraint. He picked up one shell and clinked it against another, as though sounding a coin, then stroked the ridges and curves with the tips of his delicate fingers, and began to push the shells around on the table, very slowly and deliberately. As he did so, Jane noticed that, for the very first time since the death of his father, he was crying, although he made no sound at all. She saw, too, that he was pushing the shells carefully into a pattern. He took his time, and when he was finished, the cold, white shells were laid out in a perfect circle. This done, he fell again to simply looking at them in silence.

Jane felt as though he had hit her hard with his fist.

She could not bear to stay in the kitchen, and although she wanted to run away, she forced herself to leave very quietly. She went out of the house and went down to the orchard.

Time and time again, she had come to a point in her life when she thought that at last she was in control: everything had changed, and everything would be all right. She had felt like this on the day she was confirmed, on the day she met James, even on the day her father-in-law died; but now she knew that nothing had changed and that nothing would ever change. Once, to realize this would have made her feel bitter and afraid, but now she felt peaceful and resigned. For the first time ever, she could accept the dignity of James having had a family, and of his having happy memories which she could never share. She respected the privacy of these memories, and felt that if he were to come out to her now and tell her the name of the resort where they had gathered the shells, or try to tell her some little anecdote about a rock pool, that she would cover her ears with her hands, and scream so that she might not hear; she would tell him that he ought to do nothing with his memories but cherish them. Even as she thought this, she felt as though she had unclenched her fist, and spread the palm wide, so that something which had been trapped there for years arose, lighter than air, lighter than light, floated, vanished, and that she was the better person for having had the courage to let go.

There is a certain futility in loving the dead, and a certain hopelessness in loving them too much. Jane remembered the strangeness of those years in the convent when she had loved so much two people who were dead, and in the moments when she was not loving them, she was trying to convince herself that they had ever existed. Jane now saw how the dead abandon the living, and that their going is a last lesson. In the face of their letting go, she too had to let go; had to meet their abandon of her by abandoning them. She would have to look to what was left to her – what was, like her, alive, and choose to love that.

She left the orchard and she went back towards the house. When she entered the farmyard, she found that James had left the kitchen, and that he was standing by the back door, leaning against the jamb. Jane went up to him, and without speaking she put her hand into his small hand. After a few moments, still tightly holding his hand, she led him out across the farmyard to the side of the house, where a hawthorn was growing. With her free hand, Jane caught hold of one of the branches, and gently pulled it down.

'Look,' she said.

She showed him something which she had found that morning, and which had touched her deeply, despite her usual revulsion for the creatures. At once she had resolved to keep the knowledge to herself, but now she was pleased at the secret she shared, and the memory she created as she made the screen of bright leaves recede, revealing to the couple a small mossy nest wedged in the crook of a branch. The nest contained three fledglings, whose red beaks gaped wide for food. They looked at them for a long time, then Jane carefully released the branch, and the nest was again hidden from sight.

The summer after the funeral was the happiest time of her life. The weather continued to be fine. They kept open the doors and windows of the house and the air, sweetened with the scent of flowers, blew through all the rooms. Jane found that her senses were heightened now, as if the death had made her more alive, her skin thinner and the impression of each smell, sight and sound was much more vivid than ever before. She found it easier to accept life in the country, and began to notice details which had previously escaped her notice. In the fold of a leaf she saw a ladybird, bright as liquid, wedged there like a drop of blood which had taken legs and life. The sound of the birds no longer had the power to frighten her, and she even found it comforting to see the little lumpish nests of house-martins stuck up under the eaves of the house. At dusk each evening she sat by an upstairs window to watch the mayflies as they drifted in hazy, mumbling clouds along the bay, like a light grey smoke.

She now felt closer to James than ever before, and no longer wanted to force him into opening his mind to her. Although often when they were together they were as silent as they had been in the strained, early days of their marriage, the silence now was easy and relaxed. (And Jane, who had learnt throughout her life all the varied qualities and textures of silence, was highly conscious of this.) When James's father died, it was as if a part of James himself had been cut away and buried. James was stronger for this, however, not weaker. He could not properly love his father now, and having no family, he found a family in Jane and she in him. She was by turns his wife, his sister, his daughter; and he to her was the brother, son and father she had never known, as well as being her husband. But there were often times when the significance which they had for each other went beyond names, when any word or label would have been a barrier, a limit and a lie, for the importance of each person to the other was beyond time, definition or language. Without any act of will or artificiality, they had come to a point where their lives and their selves were so bound up together that mere physical distance from each other meant nothing. When James was out working in the fields, or away at a market in the next town, Jane no longer fretted about him as she once might have done. A field or a few miles of countryside could not part them in any important sense.

All that summer, it was obvious that Ellen and Gerald were unhappy together. Jane said nothing, but hoped that things would improve for them. Thinking back to how bad her own marriage once had been, she hoped that she and James would never again feel so distant from each other, for she did not think that she would be able to bear that again.

Sometimes Jane would make a great effort to be fully conscious of the passage of time. She counted the days, the weeks, the months since the death, noted her precise age as a little child might do, and watched her own life pass. And she noted these things with such particular care, because on other occasions it was a matter of total indifference: time meant nothing at all. The sensation of this came most clearly to her one afternoon in late summer. She had fallen asleep in an armchair in the kitchen, and when she awoke, for a few moments her life was completely without context. She did not know if she was in bed beside her husband or not, did not know the time of day or night, nor the year nor the season. She could have been a child, a single woman, a wife or a widow, and it did not seem to her to have a jot of importance. A moment later, when she came to full consciousness, it was like birth; like falling out of nothingness to a precise point in time and space, as if her whole life had been sublimated so that she came from birth to this place in time with a complete personal history, like a gift which had been given to her. It was as though her past was not something which she had lived, but which was a story put in her mind to placate her, and to make her be – or appear to be – like other people. She lay back in the chair and she closed her eyes, protecting herself for a few moments from time and action.

Near to the house there was a hedge, and she had watched it all that summer, as though it were a slow clock which showed the seasons instead of the hours. The hedge was made of hawthorn, thick and laced through with ivy, bindweed and briars. The briars grew throughout the summer so fast and so long that one could almost see them growing, and they at first bore flowers; pinkish pale flowers which faded and left hard, green fruit, which grew bigger, reddened, grew softer and darker, until they were black and rotting upon the hedge. The air became colder and the nights began to close in. Leaves faded and fell, and all the apples in the orchard ripened and grew big. Some fell to earth one night in a storm, but many more remained until the trees were bare of leaves and only the fruit was left, hard and green and bright. The shooting season began again. And when the autumn wore into winter, Jane thought of how she forgot each season as soon as it was over. At the height of summer, it was inconceivable that there should ever again be deep snow in the orchard, and in winter she found it hard to imagine summer's heat. Nothing was real but the present moment. For the first time in her life she did not dread the coming of winter.

And towards the end of that year, she told James that she was going to have a baby.

CHAPTER SIX

Now it is February; now it is night. Catherine wakes in darkness and in pain, but neither disturb her as she is used to both. The pain is acute and she steadies her breathing, tries to distract her mind by concentrating on a memory, as others might recite a rhyme for the sake of its simple rhythm. Perhaps if she clings hard to the memory, it will pull her up out of the pain.

In her mind, Catherine is a child again. She is sitting in the orchard with her mother and sister, and they are playing cards: Snap, Old Maid, Happy Families. All the cards have floral designs on their backs, and each pack has a different coloured background: red, green, blue. Their mother is happy and laughing. She is wearing a white cotton dress with a wide skirt, which is overprinted with a black lattice and huge pink roses. But the woman's face is a blur, and although the scene is a memory (it is not something which Catherine has dreamt or imagined) her mother's face has that mysterious quality of a face in a dream. She can see that she is laughing but she cannot see her face, has remembered everything, even the fact of her mother's happiness and laughter: but the face she has forgotten.

Their father is there too. He is not playing cards, but he creeps around behind the children, looking at everyone's hands and whispering advice in the children's ears on the strength of what he sees, helping them to cheat until they realize that he is fooling them too, playing all three women off against each other. By this time he has brought the game to a point of hopeless confusion, and the cards fly into the air as they pounce on him, beating and tickling him until he roars for mercy. Then they all fall breathless upon the grass, while the light dapples through the branches of the trees.

And as the memory breaks over Catherine of their exploding upon their father, shrieking and pummelling him, she feels again the joy of that time, and is about to cry aloud when the pain intensifies. It stabs sharply then fades away; and as it goes the bright scene in the orchard also fades, as though it were a picture worked in stained glass, and night is falling, bleeding away the colour.

Catherine remembers little of her childhood, and she feels that she has lost those years as absolutely as one might lose a stone in the long green grass of a field. Catherine sometimes finds things when she is out walking: marbles of coarse green glass which once stoppered bottles; fragments of blue pottery, pieces of clay pipe; and she wonder now if her memories are lost only to her, wonders if perhaps in years to come someone will find and preserve them: perhaps make sense of them and understand them as she has never been able to understand the fact of their absence.

She can hear the night rain beat down upon the slates as she thinks of an alternative to this forgetfulness. What if it were impossible to forget, so that she remembered everything with such clarity that the memory became life itself? Memory then would be no comfort but a trap, forcing her to live again and again things that should be long past. To have such a faculty would mean that lying here in bed would be to lie as in a coffin, with the past shovelled on to her, as heavy and as dark as six foot of soil. When she remembers her mother's death, she is grateful for her fallible memory; more grateful still when she thinks of other memories, quite recent, and so discomforting that her mind shies away from them even in their imperfection. The thought of the mark on her sister's neck brings with it other thoughts and things remembered. If only now she could get rid of her last few memories and truly have a mind as blank as she pretends it is, perhaps she could be happy. All memory lost! She feels angry for failing to be honest even with herself, even in the privacy of her own mind, at night, in the blackness, for while her memory is poor, she has not forgotten everything; oh yes, she still remembers much.

The pain returns, as if in punishment for her failure to see things honestly, to look as if she truly wanted to understand, no matter how much the truth will hurt her. The orchard flutters again (cards, grass, a lattice of flowers and light), fades and is gone, and the pain goes too. She breathes deeply and turns upon her side.

She thinks now, *I could kill the goat*. In spring the goat is out in the field, stretching itself to the end of its tether to eat a perfect circle of grass. But Catherine thinks that perhaps the only way to solve her problem would be to kill the goat.

She would say to her sister, 'Look'. She would lead the creature into the farmyard, look for a moment into its crafty eyes, and then slit its throat. She would cut open its belly and pour its hot purple entrails out upon a flat stone, play to the full the part of the eccentric holy woman. Then she would poke through the entrails and speak the words of the haruspex, the craftiness of the dead goat going into herself. She would say then what she had seen elsewhere, say it without any crossing of a palm with silver, and with the accuracy of knowledge which no other fortune teller could provide. It was too much to hope that her sister would be impressed with this gift. Perhaps later she would be amazed, and when the shock of what she was told had worn off, she would think with wonder of the feat which her sister had performed. And Catherine would tell Sarah nothing but the truth. She always told her the truth: when she told her anything.

The slyness was that when one spoke the words aloud, one did not necessarily look at the same sign where one had first read or interpreted the truth. But what of that? Did it make such a difference that Catherine could tell the future by seeing the past, by looking at a pair of hands pulling on oars, rather than by looking at a pile of entrails?

But why should I have to be the one to tell her? Perhaps she will never forgive me for that. She will be shocked at her own stupidity. Why has she not also guessed long before now? A more sinister thought now comes to Catherine: perhaps Sarah *has* guessed the truth, but chooses to ignore it. Catherine quashes the idea at once. No, Sarah cannot know. Neither of them know. But because I know, I am guilty. If anything happens it will be my fault for denying the truth of the past. I will be the one who allowed time to repeat things which are wrong.

Catherine knows her punishment. Because she denies the past, she is denied a future. She has a vision – not a memory or a dream, or a thought, but a vision – and she has been surprised to find that her sister also has such a vision which comes to her mind again and again, often at the most unexpected times. It comes without any feeling of emotion or desire. A war has torn the whole world asunder but for one country, and in that last remaining country is her last remaining friend, the last person who cares for her. In her vision Sarah crosses that continent, crosses water and risks danger, is without food or sleep or money, and she comes at last, wounded and dirty and tired, to the house of the person whom she had sought. And at that house she is welcomed and washed and fed and forgiven, and then left to sleep upon a couch.

'And then what?' Catherine had asked.

'And then: nothing. That's all there is,' her sister replied.

But Catherine can never reciprocate, because her vision is much more sinister. As with Sarah's, it comes to mind unbidden and seemingly without reason: but no. Again she must be honest. This vision does come at a particular time: it comes when she tries to look into her own future. Catherine finds herself looking down what ought to be a sculpture gallery, where there should be symmetrical rows of marble busts upon wooden plinths, dark paintings in heavy gilt frames, a marble floor and a high vaulted ceiling of wood. But instead there is nothing at all: only the horror of a bright white light from which she cannot escape. She cannot close her eyes or turn away, for the light is still there. This light and this emptiness is her punishment and her future. Tomorrow will come: she will peel potatoes and milk the cows and find that she can do nothing to break through the loneliness of her father and sister, and when she goes back into her own mind she knows that she will find there no comfort for the future. She will find nothing there but this unbearable light. When she remembers this, the prayer which they say for her mother, asking that perpetual light may shine upon her, seems like no prayer at all and no blessing, but the most terrible curse.

Catherine is not fully convinced of her mother's immortality. She cannot imagine or conceive of a place or a state where she now might be. Catherine has come to the limits of her orthodox religion: she cannot believe in resurrection. She can only hope that somewhere her mother still exists, and that she is at peace; but if Catherine was forced to choose, she would rather see her annihilated than omniscient. She does not know how her mother could ever be at rest if she knew what Catherine knows, and if she could really see what Catherine can only see by implication and imagination. She fears the nothingness of pure light; but in her greatest fear she feels close to her mother, for she, too, must be in a state of utter timelessness, beyond place and pain, if she is anywhere at all. Every day in her life Catherine is conscious of the emptiness of light, and she struggles against it. Her diary is a proof, at least to herself, that she still has a life, but she dreads the day that will come when she will have nothing to write, not even the unhappy things with which she now fills the pages, together with casual notes of when the swallows come and go, and the date of when the lilacs begin to fade. The day will come when she will have nothing to write, not even the word 'nothing', and thereafter will be an unfinished book, all the pages blank. It frightens her even to imagine the whiteness of each succeeding sheet of paper, and she thinks that thumbing through the blank leaves will be like looking in a mirror, only to find that one had no reflection.

At what precise point of time did this happen? When did she lose her future? *When the nuns turned me down for the convent,* she thinks. She sees herself on that day last autumn, waiting in the neat little parlour, and thinking with pleasure that soon this will be her new home. The Mistress of Novices enters. Nothing could have prepared Catherine for the shock of refusal. Not this year, but perhaps next: 'We'll see then.' We'll see. Words to use to placate a child, words that mean 'No'. Treated in this way Catherine becomes petulant as a child, answering, 'We'll see' with 'You promised!' The sister almost smiles, but she looks very sad and she is utterly intransigent

'They don't want me,' Catherine says that night when she walks into the back scullery. Sarah looks up from the pan in which she is frying eels.

'Why not?' she asks.

'I don't know.'

The smell and the heat of the eels fills the scullery, so that the very air feels greasy. Sarah wipes her hands on her apron.

'Perhaps next year,' she says.

'That's what the nuns said,' Catherine replies, 'but I don't believe it.'

Sarah pokes in the pan with a long fork. 'I'm really sorry, Catherine.'

Catherine does not believe this either.

She did not cry then, but she cries now at the memory of it, and propping herself up on her elbow, she reaches under the pillow for a handkerchief. Finding it, she wipes her eyes and lies down again, but she can think only of Sarah's opposition to her, and she can only cry to think of it.

She remembers a day the previous July. She is standing in the farmyard and Sarah is at a slight distance from her, near to the water butt at the side of the byre. As is her custom now that she knows she is leaving, Catherine closes her eyes and tries to keep in her mind an accurate image of the scene before her. As always she fails, for on looking again, what she sees is slightly but significantly different from what she had for an instant remembered. After a few moments, she walks over to Sarah who does not acknowledge her presence, but continues trailing her fingers through the soft green scum on the water of the butt.

'I won't be here this time next year,' she says.

'Lucky you,' replies Sarah flatly.

But when Catherine begins to say how difficult it will be for her to leave, her sister interrupts, speaking quietly, 'You want to leave us and you want that more than anything else, so don't try to pretend otherwise. Mama's dead, and now you're going to break up the little that's left of that family to which you like to pay such great lip-service. It'll not really be a family after you've gone, but that doesn't matter, does it? Nothing matters except that you have your own way, so as to save your own soul. Isn't that right?' She does not pause to allow Catherine to justify her actions, but she continues speaking and she continues stroking the slimy surface of the water. 'Christ said that He came to divide families, didn't He? Something about not bringing peace on earth but a sword, and setting parents against children and children against parents. I'm sure that you know the details better than I do. In which case, you're only doing as He said. You must feel very proud, Catherine.'

But when she lifts her head and looks at her sister, the most painful thing to Catherine is not the distance of anger and misunderstanding that there is between them, but the closeness which she feels. For when Catherine looks at Sarah, she sees herself divided. It is as if all the doubts and misgivings which she had tried so hard to suppress and ignore have been exorcised from her and cast into another, physically identical woman, and that other self is now standing before her, demanding justification. There is nothing for Catherine to say.

The only possible comfort she can feel as Sarah walks away from her, is that if she shares so perfectly the misgivings Catherine has, then surely, deep down, she must also feel Catherine's conviction, must understand what her sister feels and desires.

This belief is confirmed towards the end of that year, when she sees the relationship develop between Peter and Sarah. Now it is in a sense too late, for it is some months since she has been refused admission to the convent, but still Catherine wants to take her sister aside and say to her, 'Now do you see what I wanted? Now do you see what I needed so much?' Religious love, sexual love, what did it matter? Just so long as it was something more than family love: something other than that. And as though to want that other love were weakness, she is comforted to see that someone else is similarly weak: she can almost feel relieved to watch her sister.

Almost. But not quite.

Catherine's religion gave her and gives her no peace. She knows that Sarah will never be happy with Peter. It is all she can do to stop herself from rising now and going to her sister's bed, wakening her and saying, 'You must stop now. It will only become worse.' Every Saturday, she watches Sarah closely when she has returned from the cottage. Sometimes she is miserable almost to the point of tears, sometimes her temper is short, never does she seem contented. *Surely*, Catherine thinks, *there must be some happiness or satisfaction to be had from the affair, or else why does she do it?* She remembers how she had tried at first to pretend that nothing was happening, but insidiously attempted to turn Sarah against Peter by reminding her of their mother's dislike of the pair at the cottage. But Sarah of course ignored all this, and went her own wilful way.

To Catherine the affair is a mystery in so many ways, and she wonders what it must feel like to open oneself to another person and be accepted, but her mind shies away when she tries to imagine the intimacy between them. She is hurt to think of their complicity. The idea that Sarah and Peter might talk about Catherine in her absence is hateful to her, until the point has come when she forces herself to ask her sister about it, no matter what the consequences might be. Sarah replies, 'Talk about you? You flatter yourself. We have better things to talk about.' The tone is teasing, but Catherine knows instinctively that she is being completely honest, and when Sarah smiles at her she is kindly, without any trace of malice. She knows that Sarah understands her worry: it is like the fear of being watched unknown while one is asleep.

Catherine turns over in bed and lies flat upon her back. She remembers hospital tests in August: naked, but for a little dress of pale blue interfacing, she lies upon a narrow couch. They are taking X-rays, and the room is full of big machines. Catherine is made to lie upon her back, and when she looks up at the ceiling, she sees a coloured poster of Piglet and Pooh; imagines sick children lying where she now lies. Look up, dear. Look at Pooh while the lady takes a photograph of what's inside you. A very special photograph.

She is alone with the nurse who makes her turn upon her side to lie coiled up, and as the woman guides her body into position, the feel of her hand upon Catherine's bare skin makes Catherine feel vulnerable and uneasy.

Five minutes later, the nurse asks her, 'Why are you crying? I can't possibly be hurting you.'

She cannot tell the simple, stupid truth. She cannot say to this strange woman, 'I'm lonely.'

In remembering this, she understands her sister, and can almost envy her.

If only she did not know. If only there was nothing to know.

But the images breed in her mind: herself crying on a plastic couch; Sarah and Peter in the cottage, and Peter and herself out in a boat.

Oars creaking in thole-pins. She looks at his hands. She raises her head and looks into the light. She will not speak to him. She does not want to speak to him ever again.

What she saw on that day has changed her whole life. It has heightened her consciousness to a degree that she can hardly bear. She remembers going back to the farm that afternoon, and she walks into the scullery feeling as though she has been flayed alive: not figuratively, but literally, so that every touch hurts. Now everything frightens her: the cups on the shelf, the farm cat licking itself at the door, the big tree opposite the house. She feels that every little thing which she sees and touches may at any moment fall apart under this new lucidity. Having seen the hidden significance in one thing, she is afraid that she will see something horrible in every simple thing.

And when Sarah took up with Peter, she could not believe the perversity of her sister: that she had to choose him, out of all people! But it was obvious that there really was no one else for her to choose.

She moves now like one lost, like one who has awoken in a strange country where the language is the language she has always spoken, but the meaning has changed. When she speaks a blessing the people understand a curse, and when she speaks of love they think she speaks of hate.

And her religion is not a comfort to her, but a torment. (Be honest, she thinks: that was the day when my future went astray, not when the nuns refused me.) It strengthened her resolve to go to the convent, but everything changed. That night when she came back from the boat, she prayed but she felt nothing. From that day on, she had no sense of the presence of God. Still she believes, but God's silence hurts her.

Now she lives with this silence and emptiness. It is like learning to live with the loss of a sense, while concealing that loss from those around her. Still she keeps hoping. The spring will come, the summer will come. Sarah will no longer want Peter. My pains will go away. Dada will content himself.

Down in the parlour cupboard, there is a delft bowl filled with soil, in which are planted five tulip bulbs and Catherine thinks of them now. She knows that they have reached the point of being five short yellow spikes, but they will continue to grow, and when they are in the light they will grow further. They will be like stiff green flames unfurling, hard and vibrantly green, and then the green flower will come and grow and the colour will blush into it; in her mind's eye the flower grows and gains colour, and she finds this promise of spring a comfort, the same comfort she feels when, on a summer evening, she sees the late light slant thick through the window and fall upon the wall in a broad gold bar; gilding the air through which it passes. When she thinks of these things, even now, in winter, in the night, she can almost persuade herself that all will be well.

CHAPTER SEVEN

At the moment when Jane's baby was born, she turned her head sharply aside to face the window, and as she felt the weight of the child slide from her body the physical pain receded. She opened her eyes and saw, through her tears, the flat lough burn up the golden light of an afternoon in early summer; the sky above the water was bleach-white. The scene was now so familiar to Jane that its very strangeness lay in its familiarity, like the sight of a loved one's half-remembered face, seen again after years of absence. She could scarcely have felt more amazed to open her eyes upon something completely unexpected; upon, say, a bright blue sea, or a forest filled with hunters and deer, than upon this stretch of predictable water.

'Don't you want to see your baby?' said the midwife's voice. 'It's a little boy.'

'No,' said Jane, and she quickly closed her eyes again upon the light of the view before her. The child had been stillborn: she had known that this would be so since the early stages of labour. Jane had resolved, even as she struggled to give birth, that she would not look at the baby.

'I don't want to see it, take it away please,' she said, her eyes still firmly closed.

But James wanted to see the child.

His presence at the confinement was precluded by the customs of that time and place, and on her arrival the midwife had bustled him out of the room. He was reluctant to leave. For some time after that he hovered around by the closed door, until the noises from within began to disturb him. The moans and half-whispers reminded him of the noises which he and Jane had once struggled to suppress so that his father would not hear them. He felt then that to listen at the door was wrong, and that he would either have to go into the room or go downstairs. For a moment he wanted to flout custom, to open the door and stay with Jane until the birth took place, if she would have him there. But his resolution wavered when he put his hand upon the doorknob: he could not bring himself to intrude upon the intimacy of what was already happening in the room, and sadly, reluctantly, he went down to the kitchen.

When the midwife told him what had happened, his first concern was for Jane. Assured of her health and safety, he then asked to see the child. The baby was brought to him and he looked at it: looked for a very long time. Then he swaddled the bundle up in his arms, and carried it upstairs. The midwife had told him of Jane's reluctance to look, but he wanted her to look too, and to be as amazed and comforted as he was. As soon as the bedroom door opened, however, and Jane caught sight of the white shawl, she hid her head under the blankets.

'Take it away from me,' she said. 'It's dead, and I won't look at it.'

'He's a lovely baby,' said James, 'and you ought at least to look at him. You'll regret it later if you don't.'

The muffled voice from under the blankets said again, 'Take it away from me. Take it away.'

James did not reply, but he left the room. When the door closed and she could hear the sound of his feet descending the stairs, Jane poked her head out above the blankets. She lay there alone for a long time, and by dusk she had drifted off into a deep and dreamless sleep.

She awoke in darkness. Night had long since fallen, and while she slept, someone had pulled the curtains and had tucked the blankets neatly up around her, but in her first moments of consciousness, this was not what Jane noticed. Instead, she felt instinctively that something was wrong, something was different, something more than the absence of James from her side. And then she realized: for months now she had been woken daily not by the light of morning, nor by a clock, nor by James calling her because it was time to rise and work: she had been roused by the baby who woke independently and, floating inside her, kicked her into consciousness. Now her body was still and quiet as an empty house; the baby was gone. Very quietly she began to cry. The bedroom door was slightly ajar, and between the noise of her sobs she could hear the steady and unbroken beat of the big clock in the hall. Time was a trap, coiled like a spring around her, and she could see a life open out beyond her, hours, days, weeks, months, years, spiralling away to her own death, and she would have to live that life.

Every point of apparent change would be just a point of variation, moving her into the next circle of her existence, which would be not quite the same as the preceding circle, but which would be a circle still. It was a long time before she slept again.

Two days later, the baby was buried: not in the family grave with his grandparents, but alone at the foot of the hill. When Jane was told this, she closed her eyes and she did not speak. She felt the last possible shred of comfort melt away from her, and she knew as a cold fact that she would never be whole again, that this final cruelty had broken something in her which could never be mended.

She came downstairs for the first time seven days later. Her body as she dressed felt curiously flat and light, but she moved much more slowly and deliberately than she had ever done during her pregnancy. When she appeared at the kitchen door James, who was sitting drinking tea at the table, looked up in surprise. He had been encouraging her to rise for some days now, but she had given no indication that she would do so. He smiled at her, but she did not return the smile. She crossed in silence to the armchair beside the stove, and sat down.

'Would you like a cup of tea? There's some left in the pot.'

She shook her head.

'Is there anything I can get for you?'

Again the same response, and then Jane fixed her gaze on a point in the middle distance, somewhere past James's head. While she looked away, James continued to drink his tea and watch her, until suddenly he realized that this was how it had all started in that café, four years ago. He wondered now what he would have said if, on that day, someone had told him of all that was to happen between them, and that yet, four years later, they would be sitting together in an identical pose, as if nothing whatever had changed, as if they were still strangers and in each other's company by mere chance of circumstance.

He remembered that day vividly and with guilt, for what had interested him first in Jane was a self-possession so complete that it withdrew all feeling and all personality from her face, and he felt that he was looking at a mask: a familiar mask. The large blue eyes, the high forehead, the pale skin: these features formed a face which was, to James, so passive and lifeless, that as he watched, he found himself grafting on a personality and a past life which belonged to someone else, but which, oddly, seemed to fit.

He was so absorbed in this task that when the young woman at last turned to him and spoke, he was shocked and quickly became confused. He knew that he had done something wrong. He engaged her in conversation and listened politely when she spoke, as though to give some credit to the reality of her personality. He remembered the horrible little tingle of fear he had felt when the woman lowered her eyes and with seeming artlessness told him the story of her life; for it was no more than a variation of the life he had given her. When she stood up to leave he felt a sense of panic: if he lost her now, for the rest of his life he would wonder if she was real, knew that soon he might believe her to be nothing more than a creature of his imagination, conjured up out of his unhappiness and loneliness. So he had quickly asked to see her again: Jane had said, 'Yes.'

Often since that day he wished that when she finished her tea and rose to leave the café, he had said no more than 'Goodbye'. Often since that day little instances of her lack of feeling had horrified him. He had tried to understand the misery of her loneliness, and the strange, sad life which had made her the woman she was. But as he looked at her now, sitting stiffly in the chair beside the stove, he knew that her new grief would do nothing to soften her. She had put herself beyond the power of his comfort, and she would keep herself rigidly there; nor could she be a comfort to him. And James felt a great sense of pity which encompassed them both as he looked at her, and remembered that they would be husband and wife until death.

In the following weeks, their lives began to get back into some semblance of order. Jane found that the routine chores of the farm allowed her to slip back into a life identical to the life which she had lived since first coming to the house. She went through many of the motions and emotions which she had experienced at the time of her father-in-law's death, and her sadness now was that the baby had left so little mark upon the house: there was so little to be done. Over a year ago she had cleared out the old man's cluttered bedroom, and had been amazed to think that all these things would never be needed again. Now, she had to dismantle the nursery which she had so carefully prepared.

She remembered sorting through her father-in-law's clothes, remembered the strange intimacy of that, for they smelt of sweat and tobacco, they were creased and the cuffs were grimy, and they would never be any more smelly, crumpled or dirty than they were then. But now she was faced with another pile of clothes to be disposed of, and although their owner was dead too, the pain here was that the clothes were all perfect, all clean, untouched, unworn. There were thick piles of soft white nappies, little jackets and hats and boots, most of which she had herself knitted, and a long white christening robe, the newness of which she resented most of all. The clothes were all so soft and tiny that it seemed ludicrous, unbelievable, that their owner could be dead. Dead people were old people, people like parents who had worn out their clothes, their bodies, their lives. Kneeling by the side of the bed, she buried her face in the heap of baby clothes, feeling their softness and wishing that they could be pervaded with the warm, milky, sexless smell of a baby, but she knew that they would never be; knew that there would never be anything more than this smell of newness and clean wool. People in the village said to her that she was young, she would have another child, but that did nothing to placate her. She could not yet bear to think of the possibility of having another baby, of going through all that long waiting again, perhaps to face at last that same sadness and disappointment. But even if she did have another baby, she knew that she would never again have *that* baby, the baby who was dead. And these clothes belonged to that baby: she felt that it would be a violation to allow another child to wear them.

One afternoon in July, she lit a fire in the yard, and then, one by one, she carefully fed each little garment into the flames. When they were all gone, she realized that the only material proof she now had that the baby had ever existed were two pieces of paper: one a birth certificate, one a death certificate. There were also some little silvery stretch marks upon her body.

James was angry about the burning of the clothes. She had thought that he might be, and so she made a point of doing it while he was out across the fields working, and also of telling him what she had done as soon as he came back to the farm. He was angry, hurt and angry; and these were the responses she had expected and desired. They were back again at the point to which they had been brought by the death of his father: they had no one but each other. Now, however, Jane did not want to cling to him, but to wound him. Since that first death she felt that they had become truly married; felt that he was a part of her and she was a part of him, and so she now wanted to hurt and wound him because she wanted to hurt and wound herself. Seeing his pain, and seeing that she worsened it, gave her a bleak form of satisfaction.

One day in July when she went out to the byre to call him for lunch, she found him weeping. She did nothing to comfort him. Although she wanted to go over to him and embrace him, wanted to do that more than anything else in the world, she beat this feeling down, and she stood there in silence, coldly watching him. She saw that he was ashamed of his tears, and that her silence only made his weeping sound the more pathetic and weak. At last, still crying, he pushed past her out of the byre and across the yard.

Jane, of course, also cried: often she would be engaged on some simple chore in the house and think that her sadness was not worse than any other time, when suddenly whatever was before her – a basin of potatoes which she happened to be peeling, or a piece of mending on which she was engaged – these things would suddenly blur and vanish before her unexpected tears. When this happened she did not seek out her husband, but fell back on the perverse strength of her childhood, and hid herself away until she had willed herself over this brief loss of face.

One morning when they were sitting in silence at breakfast, James suddenly said to Jane, 'It's not my fault that the baby died, you know. I'm not to blame.'

Jane did not reply. The tense atmosphere was not eased by the arrival of Gerald some moments later. Without him ever saying so, it was evident throughout that summer that his own marriage with Ellen was proving to be intensely unhappy. Jane noticed this, but it barely surprised her, and she did not care. Her own misery kept her fully occupied, and the same was true of James, who did not have the necessary strength both to bear his loss and to humour Jane. Perhaps he did not realize that she needed to be humoured, for he did not understand the nature of her grief, did not understand that she was translating it into anger and deflecting it on to him. Her anger, her coldness, her sullenness made James feel hurt and resentful. By the time summer was at its height, relations between them were worse than they had ever been before.

Jane's resentment of her husband grew in proportion to her regret that she had not looked at the child; and that regret grew fast, until it soon reached the point of obsession. Night after night she would dream about the baby. In her dreams the child was sitting upon her lap and facing away from her, but when she tried to make him turn his head, the child strongly resisted. At last she would succeed, only to find nothing: only to find that the front of the child's head was as blank as that of a tailoress's dummy. She began to cry, and then the faceless baby vanished.

She envied James because he had looked at the baby, and hated herself because she had not. She was too proud to ask him to describe the child to her, and also too wretched. She knew that no matter what he said, it would never be enough; that the mystery would always remain, and there was no one she could blame for this but herself. Even with this knowledge, she spent hours leafing through a book about childcare, looking intently at each of the photographs. Once, she even went to the city on the pretext of making a shopping trip, but she spent the day walking around, looking at all the babies and trying to imagine the variations necessary in each face to create the face of her own lost child. It was, of course, a futile exercise, and left her frustrated and unhappy.

She was deeply hurt, too, by the child's exclusion from the family grave, and his relegation to the patch of ground at the foot of the hill In the course of that summer, she spent many hours thinking about this. She realized that she would never be buried with her child unless she took her own life.

One night she could not sleep, and lay awake for hours beside James. She thought about the baby: once, it had had a place in time. As she listened to James's steady breathing, she remembered the time after his father's death when they had been happy together, remembered the nights of the preceding summer, during one of which the baby had been conceived, and tried to understand how the child had passed so quickly from that physical reality to its present state. She wanted to understand this as far as she possibly could, and rising from the warmth of the bed, she left the room. Barefoot and wearing only her thin nightdress, Jane went downstairs and passed through the empty house, opened the back door and walked out into the night. She stopped in the middle of the yard, and turned her face away from the lough shore, on the far side of which she could see a few yellow lights twinkle; turned too from the house. Instead, she put back her head and looked up at the sky, which was moonless and starless and black. She tried to imagine the baby in just such a blackness, but this was not a void, and she could not properly imagine a soul beyond help, beyond time, beyond reach, for she could feel a light breeze upon her face and the ground under her feet was hard and cold; the leaves rustled in the orchard and she could hear the cries of the birds; when she breathed in, she could smell the earth's dampness. Then she knew that she would never be able to take her own life, that it was a thing too terrible and too sacred. Death did not end life, it merely changed it. She knew that she would never be able to believe anything other than this. The baby was still real, but it was in a reality outside time.

For the rest of that summer, Jane waited. She knew what was going to happen, but did not know the precise moment when the consciousness of everything around her would overwhelm her completely. James, in retrospect, would think that during that summer she had withdrawn into herself, that she had cut herself off from the world, when in fact the exact opposite was true. Never before had she felt so vulnerable and open to the mere existence of other things. When she looked at an animal or a flower, her own identity dissolved and flowed out, so that she could hardly tell where she, Jane, ended, and the cat or the rose began. Her mind felt raw as a wound, every thought a touch that hurt. The presence of Gerald and James did not really register with her, but she watched obsessively all the natural things around her. She waited for summer to end and the autumn to come, longing for this to happen, even though the knowledge of what it would bring frightened her.

All the flowers in the garden died, and the air at night became cool and sharp. She watched the swallows as they crowded along the telegraph wires, strung out like plain-chant against the white sky. Jane watched them do this for several days, and then one morning she awoke to find the wires all bare, for the birds had flown away. She felt completely abandoned.

Later that day, she accidentally broke a white dinner plate. It cracked cleanly in two, and she held up the two halves in her hands, looking at them as though they were the first things she had understood in months.

When James returned from the cottage that evening, he found that the farm was apparently deserted. He looked for Jane in every room, then searched around the farm-yard, but he did not find her. He went back into the house and was standing in the kitchen wondering what to do next, when he heard a noise in the hallway. He listened again, and it led him to the cupboard under the stairs, where he found her curled up with her hands across her face. She would not look at him, and she would not speak. When he tried to make her leave the cupboard, she resisted him strongly.

Until the year had almost ended, they kept her in an asylum which reeked of disinfectant and polish. James visited her frequently, and for the first month Jane treated him as she had on the day when he found her under the stairs, refusing either to look at him or to speak. The doctors told him that she wanted to stay in darkness and silence at all times, and cried like a child when she was forced into the light or was questioned.

After a few weeks, her condition appeared to improve. She became more tractable, and when James visited she would talk with him, although with excessive politeness and formality. The treatment she received made her forgetful, and James found it upsetting, frightening even, when she failed to remember things which he had told her on earlier visits.

'You must be making a mistake,' she would say quietly. 'You never told me that before now.' And to humour her he would tell it all again, only to find on successive visits that she had still no recollection of his conversations. Once she became angry, and said that he was deliberately telling her lies to try to confuse her, and thereafter he gave in to her completely: yes, it was he who was forgetful; no, he had never told her such and such a thing until now. But it did frighten him to talk to her and see her watch him as though with piercing clarity, while knowing that she was absorbing nothing of what was being said to her. He was told that she had become very religious, so he was surprised when she said, 'Before I come home, I want you to take down all the holy pictures in the house, and put them away somewhere that I won't find them.' James promised that he would do this, and the following week she again made the same request and again he made his promise, although he had already put all the pictures and statues up in the attic. Jane frowned and pressed her palms together. 'They might let me home in time for Christmas, if I'm a good girl,' she said, with such extreme artlessness that James, knowing Jane, could not help but believe the remark was veined with irony, her illness notwithstanding.

'That would be good, wouldn't it?' he said.

'Yes.' She paused for a moment, then said again, 'You will put the pictures away before I get home, won't you?'

'Yes, of course.'

'I had a dream and it was very hot, I was suffocating and the pain, you wouldn't believe the pain, I was all sweating and blood and the pain, there were little flies all around my face and I couldn't brush them away, my eyes kept closing and I knew that if I didn't keep them open I would close them once and never open them again.' Again she was silent, and twisted her palms together. 'Before Christmas. Perhaps. If I'm good.'

Exactly a week before Christmas, James collected Jane and took her home. As they drove up towards the farm, they saw Ellen in the distance, and making no comment, Jane instinctively turned her head aside, and did not look up again until they had driven past the woman. She did not see, therefore, that Ellen was pregnant. James had not dared to tell her this while she was ill, and the sight of Ellen on the road had terrified him until he saw Jane pointedly look away. Still, he dreaded the day when she would find out. She was bound to know eventually.

As they drew up at the door of the farm, Jane was thinking of the day when first she came to the house, when she had been startled by the clamour of the wild birds, for she had expected only silence. The wildness of the landscape had frightened her, but in the years which had passed since that day she had been frightened even more by that which she had found in herself. She felt ashamed to think that she had been that stupid girl, who had come to the house with all her hopes and her expectations. She did not believe that a single illusion was left, and she was grateful for that.

'Are you glad to be home?'

'Yes.'

Jane walked through all the rooms of the house, touching things and smelling them, looking pointedly at the rectangles of unfaded wallpaper where the holy pictures had been hanging, but she made no comment.

She went to bed early that night, for she was very tired. James soon followed her, and found that she was already lying tucked up. He undressed and got into bed beside her, leaning over to kiss her in a rather hesitant way upon the cheek. Her skin smelt of soap.

'I'm so glad that you're home and that you're well again,' he said.

She smiled and settled down stiffly, lying far from him at the edge of the bed. After he put out the light, however, she said, 'Give me your hand please.' And when he did she gripped it tightly. They fell asleep thus, hand in hand and side by side, lying flat in the dark, as a dead knight and his lady carved in stone might lie upon their tomb for centuries, in the still and silent darkness of an empty chapel.

CHAPTER EIGHT

On an icy spring morning, when the trees are still bare and black, Lent begins. Early on Ash Wednesday morning, the family goes to church, although Sarah goes with reluctance. She sits upon a hard pew beneath a stained glass window, which is the finest of the few such windows in the chapel. She has realized that long before now, and this morning her eyes are drawn to it again and again. The window depicts the baptism of Jesus in the river Jordan, and Sarah is struck by its coolness. The morning sun catches the white dove and freezes it in its clear glass nimbus. More remarkable still is the coldness of the blue glass water and the paler blue of the pointed, sectioned sky. The coldness of the water seems inevitable, a stunning coldness, felt that morning in the icy bathroom where she washed, and again in the chapel's damp porch, dipping her fingers in the grimy water of the dark stone font. And an image suddenly rises in her mind of the man, all those years ago, walking out into the lough secretly to give himself up forever to the water's coldness, and Sarah shivers in horror, wonders if the world will ever be warm again.

She regrets that she has come to the church, for here the sadness and exhaustion which she has lately felt cannot be fought, but instead gathers together and intensifies. All around her are the familiar faces of people from the village, and sitting near by are Ellen and Peter. He catches her eye but no flicker of recognition, much less affection, passes between them. Remembering that it is mid-week, Sarah feels more miserable still, as she thinks of the dull days since last she was with Peter, and of the days still to be lived until she will be free to go to him again. He kneels, and from where she is sitting, Sarah looks down upon the fair crown of his bowed head, and wonders at his passivity; remembers the feel of his mouth acquiescent upon her mouth, and the warm weight of his hand lying in the small of her back, to which point she had guided it.

One by one, the people go up to the altar and the priest smears ash upon their foreheads. Sarah watches them as they come down by the side aisle. She does not want to go up, but then when her sister stirs beside her and leaves the pew, Sarah follows her at once, with instinctive solidarity, for she cannot let Catherine do this alone.

When she feels the cold thumb of the priest upon her forehead Sarah thinks for a moment that she will faint, for it is like the touch of death itself. She feels as if coldness and eternal silence are being pressed into her mind, as if her dead mother has returned to stand secretly, silently behind her daughter, placing her slim dead hands over Sarah's eyes. Later, Sarah will not remember how she made her way back to the pew: but she will never forget the sight of the dark mark upon her sister's face. She wants to wipe the ash away and to weep, to put her arms around Catherine's neck and to console her; although Catherine's eyes are innocent still.

They return home, and the remainder of that day is taken up with the usual farm tasks, which Sarah helps her father to perform with an even greater want of interest than is usual. In the back scullery, Catherine prepares the three frugal, meatless meals required to keep the fast day. It is almost a relief when dusk begins to fall, and with it comes the rain. Sarah stands by an uncurtained window watching the water stream icily down the glass. All the chores of the day are over, but the complete weariness which she feels is due not to hard physical labour, nor to the want of food. From where she stands, she can hear a bird crying out in the blackness, like a thing without hope. Sarah will not go to bed for hours yet, knowing from past experience that this weariness is not eased by lying down but worsened.

When she thinks of her family, she wonders why all this has happened, and at times during the day she has looked from her father to her sister, as if she might see there the cause of all their misery. Or more than a cause: Sarah wants guilt and blame, wants to point the finger at someone to say, 'It's your fault: you did this.' At some point in the past, someone must have done something of their own free will, which eventually set the world unwinding around them all, and against which they can do nothing but suffer and be. But even as she thinks, she knows that it is cowardly and foolish; and that her pain comes only from consciousness of the pain around her. As she stands here by the window and looks at one particular raindrop, she knows that if she looked long enough and hard enough, in time a point would come when she would see everything in it, and would be forced to close her eyes.

In the evenings now, she withdraws early from her family's company. She cannot bear to be with them, because she is afraid that she will crack under the weight of what she knows, and that she will suddenly say it aloud, feeling that if she says it before her father and sister it will somehow make it unreal and untrue, as saying it before strangers somehow seals and confirms its reality. They cannot know yet: they cannot yet have guessed: their unhappiness must be centred around some other source. The harm that I could do, she thinks. And she fears that she will do that harm, her knowledge gives her such power. And suddenly there on that cold wet night, anger rises up in her, anger that this knowledge has been given to her, for she did not want to know, and she fears the responsibility which it puts upon her. For what if, in years to come, she will see that she waited too long to speak, and that she should not have held this knowledge a secret. Perhaps even now, with the best will possible, she is taking the worst course of action. She can confide in no one, and the strain of this loneliness is becoming too much to bear. Vividly she remembers a day one summer, years before: Catherine and herself in the loft of the barn and Catherine opens the door which gives on to nothing but the ground some twenty feet below. Beyond her sister's head she can see the sky, and she feels dizziness and fear, as if she were the one hanging on the edge of the void, and not Catherine. Crossing the loft softly, so as not to startle her sister, she gently puts her hands upon her shoulders to draw her back, but as soon as she has touched the thin warm body her resolve changes, and she feels now not the desire to save her sister, but an urge to push her out through the door, making her fall crack like an egg on the ground below. And now Sarah feels that she has that power, and is conscious of that power for every single second of the day, and she presses her forehead against the glass, believing that she cannot endure this power for a single day longer.

That night, she barely sleeps. Long before dawn she rises, packs a small bag and puts all her loose money and her savings account book in her pocket, then goes to her father's bedroom.

'Dada?'

'Mmnm?'

'I'm going to the city for the day. Tell Catherine when she rises that I'll see her this evening.'

He grunts again. The musky male smell of the room makes her think, briefly, of Peter. She goes downstairs, and, on reflection, scribbles a note in case her father on waking does not remember her visit. Then she leaves the house, walks to the village and takes the bus to the city; and once in the city she walks to the train station.

She has missed the first train east. It left an hour before her arrival, and there will not be another one for an hour and a half, so she buys her ticket and sits down on a bench to wait, with her luggage at her feet. The station is cold and bleak. Sarah considers buying a cup of tea as she did not have breakfast before leaving the house, but decides that she ought to be careful with her money: she has very little and it will have to last indefinitely. When she thinks this, she sees suddenly the strangeness and stupidity of what she is doing, and she is stricken with panic. She knows no one in the big city in the east to which she intends to travel, and she has no idea at all of what she will do or where she will go when she gets there. She sees the futility of trying to run away, but she does not leave the station, she stays rooted to the bench.

After an hour, she can wait no longer, and so she rises to go and buy a cup of tea, but as soon as she is on her feet she goes automatically not to the buffet, but to a phone booth, and she dials her home number. She hears the phone ringing, and then it is interrupted by bleeps which indicate that someone has picked up the receiver and that she is now to put in her money. Instead, Sarah panics, and hastily hangs up. Then she does go to the buffet, and she buys some tea and biscuits.

She sits on a seat of rigid orange plastic, and she warms her hands around the plastic cup. Catherine will have risen by now, she will be baffled by the scrawled note, and Sarah feels guilty at not having seen her before she left – not even having called into her room but then, Sarah has felt guilty about Catherine for some time now. She has felt guilty since the day she betrayed her by going to the convent. (And try as she might, she cannot but think of that as a betrayal.)

She will never forget that day. She thinks of it now: and she is standing again on the steps, she has rung the bell and has heard it clang in the distance, she is looking at the brass plate with ivy around it and she is almost hoping that no one will answer (a foolish hope) when she hears feet approaching within, and the heavy wooden door is swung open. Sarah asks to see the Mistress of Novices, and she waits in the dim hallway while the nun who has opened the door goes in search of her. There is a smell of floor polish, and a more distant smell of cooking vegetables. Sarah feels ill at ease in such a place, feels that her very presence contaminates it. It is bodiless, spiritual, clean; and to think that her own twin sister wishes to spend the rest of her life here shows already the distance that there is between them.

She walks across the small hallway, and looks to her left down a long corridor which is shiny and dark. The floor is highly polished, and the vaulted ceiling is of varnished wood. At intervals along one side there are holy statues: garish, ugly things. There is a big red statue of the Sacred Heart, a blue and white one of Our Lady of Lourdes, and a cream and brown one which Sarah cannot identify, for the corridor is dim. The wall facing the statues is hung with thick curtains from floor to ceiling, and chinks of daylight show between them. Sarah guesses that behind the windows which are covered by the curtains there must be a garden, for she can see a glimpse of green, and she hears the sound of bird-song. Suddenly she hears something else: the sound of footsteps behind her.

When she turns around, the Mistress of Novices smiles, as most people smile when they meet Sarah, having first met Catherine, for the physical similarity between the twin sisters is remarkable. The nun then knows immediately of whom Sarah has come to speak, but she does not know why. She takes the girl into a tiny parlour to the left of the hallway, and they sit down on a small sofa. This room has the same air of cleanliness which Sarah has already noticed. Above the mantelpiece she sees a small watercolour, and she lets her glance come to rest on that. It shows a flat landscape with a cottage and some trees, and has been executed with a fair degree of skill. The pale clouds upon the painted sky are particularly attractive. It is, she thinks, probably the work of one of the sisters in the convent, and Sarah looks at this painting very intently as she begins to speak, and she looks steadily as she has lately looked at the pen-holder upon the doctor's desk.

Then she had been listening, not speaking, and she had looked at the pen-holder which he has had for years; all her life when she has come to this surgery with her insignificant ailments she has noticed the pen-holder. It is made of plastic, and inside there are a sea-horse and some tiny shells arranged in the form of a flower. As a child she had admired it, even coveted it, but as she grew older she had wondered at the doctor having such a cheap trinket upon his desk. She wondered at the depth of sentiment that could make him keep such a thing so prominently placed before him. Or perhaps it was just habit. He never used the pen which stuck out of it, perhaps he had even stopped noticing it years ago, and would be surprised if someone pointed out to him that the ugly little thing was there upon his desk. On that day she had thought about none of these things, it had meant nothing to her. It was a thing upon which she looked, but looked as though it were an object of monumental significance; as if she were pouring her whole life and her consciousness into it, and she did this because the truth of what the doctor was saying was incredible, too shocking and too horrible to be borne. And the only truth which she had to set in the face of this was the existence of an ugly little plastic pen-holder.

The doctor thought that she was strong and brave. He had spoken directly and simply and he had not been so foolish as to try to spare her feelings by talking around the subject, as Sarah now tries to protect the nun, staring at the watercolour and talking such nonsense that she sees at last she is not trying to spare the other woman, she is trying to spare herself. The Mistress of Novices is now confused, and still looking at the painting Sarah forces herself to try to tell the simple truth, which can be told in four words. She breaks her half-spoken sentence, she breathes deeply and she says, 'My sister is . . . my sister is . . .'

She cannot speak the word. This happened before, on a morning now two years ago, when they had returned from the hospital before the dawn, and had waited until a later hour before phoning the priest to make arrangements. Even then she had apologized for phoning him so early, and had listened to her own voice, polite, almost incidental, as if she had called him for no particular reason, and then when she started to say the words, 'My mother is . . . my mother is . . .' her voice had broken and she could not speak. She could not say the word then and she had begun to cry, as she cannot say the word now and as she now begins to cry. The watercolour landscape blurs, splinters, vanishes in blackness as she closes her eyes, and the nun knows now, as the priest had known then.

'My child,' says the nun, 'my poor, poor child.' And when she puts her arms around Sarah's shoulders Sarah falls across the little sofa, crying like the child the nun has named her. She weeps, knowing that this is not an end of suffering but a beginning, that the worst is yet to come; it is all before them.

Sarah insists from the first that Catherine is to be told nothing of this visit; above all that she is not told of the intelligence which Sarah has brought with her. The Mistress of Novices questions this at first, and asks if Catherine has not got a right to such knowledge. Sarah hesitates, as she will hesitate for weeks and weeks to come, wondering at her own right to withhold this knowledge from her sister. Then she says resolutely, 'No. She must not know. At least, not yet.' Perhaps a time will come when it will be easier to tell her, or when she will guess for herself, and Sarah will only have to give confirmation and comfort. In any case, the doctor has told her not to tell her yet, that the time will come and that until then Catherine is not to be worried or stressed. The nun at last agrees.

Sitting there in the tranquil parlour, the two women make their pact of what is to be done and not done; what is to be said and not said: together they construct a future. When she is ready the nun takes her into the hallway and asks her if she would like to visit the chapel before she leaves. Sarah at once refuses, and she sees the surprise and hurt on the face of the nun, who had thought her question a formality. Already she has half-turned to go down the dim corridor, but Sarah stands her ground. 'No,' she says again, and then more quietly, 'I don't want to go: not now. Please don't force me.'

'I wouldn't dream of it,' says the nun, ever so slightly arch, but then she puts her arm around Sarah and kisses her before opening the heavy door and ushering the girl out into the street's brightness.

Sarah walks away through the city, feeling more guilty than she has ever done before in all her life. She goes into a public park and sits for a while upon a bench. Summer is ending, but still there are flowers, and the air is light and scented. People are walking back and forth, laughing and talking in the sunshine, and Sarah can hear music from a distant bandstand. As she sits there she opens and closes her eyes several times: closes them when the sight of all this life which is to be lost becomes too much for her to bear; opens them again when she can no longer tolerate the blackness.

When she goes back to the farm that night, she feels so guilty that she can scarcely look her sister in the face. Catherine is putting the dinner out on the table when Sarah walks in, and when she looks up with her mild, trusting eyes Sarah at once looks away, thinking that now she knows what it must feel like to commit adultery. For the rest of that evening she covertly looks at Catherine until she cannot bear it, then looks away until the lack of her sister is unbearable, and she is forced to look back. Catherine, sitting reading by the fire, is lonelier than she knows, and she is twice betrayed. Her own deepest secret is being withheld from her, and Sarah wonders how she would feel if the same thing were done against her. She believes that she would never be able to forgive such an act. Sarah broods on the new sisterhood she has forged that afternoon, the sister in Christ and the sister in blood making a complicity from which Catherine is excluded, conspiring about that which concerns her most deeply.

Over six months have passed since Sarah went to the convent, and still Catherine does not know. It seems that her decline has been slowed by her ignorance, for she is too preoccupied by other things to guess what is happening to her. It is the strain of waiting for that inevitable moment of revelation that has driven Sarah from her home.

Her tea has gone cold before her. She hears a shrill whistle below: she has missed the second train to the east.

By now it is noon. She waits for another hour, then she goes again to the telephone booth and she dials her home number. Again, she is on the point of getting through when she replaces the receiver. As she walks slowly back to the bench, she imagines the scene to which she has almost linked herself, imagines the life of the farm which is going on without her, for the lives of her father and sister are not dependent upon her presence or even her existence. Dada will by now be in from the fields, he will have finished his lunch and Catherine will be down in the back scullery. Sarah can see the scullery and the kitchen, she can smell the gas and dampness; Dada slitting his eyes against the smoke of his own cigarette, Catherine leaning against the steel sink and winding a coil of her hair around her index finger. *What need have they of me*? she thinks, and she knows the dishonesty of this: if it were true, she would not have had to steal away under cover of darkness.

She goes back to the buffet, and she buys another cup of tea. As she drinks it, she looks at the other people, realizing gradually how little they mean to her.

For the third time, she goes to the phone booth and dials her number, this time forcing herself not to hang up, and when the ringing noise is cut, she convulsively pushes the coin into the slot.

'Sarah? Is that you? Was it you who tried to phone earlier today?'

'Yes,' she says, and she listens now not so much to what her sister is saying as to the sound of her voice, so intimate and familiar, but weird, too, as a voice at a seance. It shocks her to hear this loved, intimate voice coming mechanical out of the filthy black receiver, as if Catherine has been refined away to nothing, as if her body has wasted, becoming thin, thinner, translucent, transparent, gone: until only a voice remains, an innocent voice which does not know the pity and grief which it provokes in Sarah.

'Sarah? Sarah? Hello, are you still there?'

'Yes.'

'I thought we'd been cut off. At what time will you be home this evening?'

'Six.'

'Are you all right, Sarah?'

'Yes.'

'Bring me some fruit, will you? Bring me some oranges.'

'Yes. I'll see you this evening.'

Three shrill pips, and the buzz of disconnection. Sarah replaces the receiver, leaves the booth wiping her eyes with the back of her hand. She has missed the latest train to the east, but that is now a matter of no importance. She throws away her ticket, and then leaves the station, walking through the rain until she comes to the city centre. She visits four fruit shops in turn, rejecting the goods of each as not being good enough, until in the fifth shop she finds what she has been looking for. She chooses and pays for twelve huge and perfectly unblemished oranges, which she puts carefully into her bag. In another shop she buys some chocolate for herself and her father, and then she wanders aimlessly around the town until it is time for her bus to leave.

On the way home, she feels both tired and foolish. How could she ever have considered seriously, even for a moment, the possibility of escaping? When she goes back to the farm, it is in a state of complete resignation, knowing that she will have to stay there until the very end. And now she wants to stay.

She is surprised by two things that evening: firstly by the conviviality of the family, for the first lambs of the year have been born that day, and they are happy about that. After dinner, they remain in the kitchen. They pull chairs round by the stove and they talk; they eat the chocolate and they peel and eat the immaculate fruit.

And she is surprised, too, to realize that when she goes up to her room that night and sees the light in Peter's window in the cottage across the fields, that it is the very first time since that morning that Peter has entered her mind at all.

CHAPTER NINE

The Christmas following Jane's illness was white, but the coming of the new year brought milder weather. There was no more snow, but throughout the month of January rain fell, persistent and heavy. At first, James took this for granted, as he took for granted Jane's silence and apparent indifference to all around her. For weeks she did little but sit by the fire, or at the window looking out at the grey curtains of rain. Reason told him that with time winter would end and Jane would recover from her depression, but it was a belief difficult to sustain in the face of her sadness and the heavy rain. Often he would wake in the night and hope to catch them both unawares; hope to find her face relaxed in sleep while a harsh, dry wind blew around the farm, but he was never successful in this. He always woke not to the stertorous sound of her breath in sleep, but to the noise of a heavy night rain beating down upon the slates, and Jane lying wide awake beside him, her eyes open and her sadness as great as ever it was in the daytime.

In time, she began to do a few household chores, and gradually did more each day. In the evenings she sewed a little or read, but always in the same dogged manner, as though she were obliged to do these things. When James watched her with her head bowed over some little piece of mending, he suddenly saw her as a child who had suffered a terrible trauma, and was now pretending to play again, although games meant nothing to her. Her silence lacked the tension of the time leading up to her illness, now she was resigned and exhausted. Still she prayed every night, but with the same air of duty which she now brought to everything she did.

One night, as she put her prayer book up on the shelf above the stove, James said, 'All the holy pictures and statues are up in the attic, from when you told me to put them away. Do you want me to bring them down again now?'

'No,' she said quickly, 'leave them where they are, please.' The matter was never mentioned again.

She met the news of Ellen's pregnancy with a shrug of indifference; and a letter telling of her aunt's death in the city elicited a similar response. She never lost her temper, and never became worked up into any state of high emotion. One day, on coming in from the farmyard, James found the kitchen empty as it had been on that day in autumn when she had fallen ill. With a mounting sense of panic, he looked for her, this time beginning with the cupboard under the stairs, but she was not there. He found her sitting in their bedroom. She made no sound at all, although the tears came from her eyes as though wrung out. When James saw her like this, he realized that what he generally saw was only the surface of her distress, was the silence and stillness in which she tried to live, protected.

In February, she began to go for long walks every day, at first insisting that she go alone. James would watch her from the window as she plodded slowly through the fields with her head bent. She brought home the things which she found: a bird's nest; fragments of a clay pipe; broken bits of blue and white delft; and tufts of sheep's greasy wool which she untangled from the barbed wire fences. Once she brought home a little glass marble with a multicoloured twist, and she stood for a long time by the window, holding it up to the light and turning it this way and that, to see how the colours changed. He asked her why she brought these things home, and she said very quietly, 'I don't know why. I just do it.'

For the first few months after her illness, they did not make love. There was no indication of any sexual feeling on her part, so much so that James did not dare show any such feeling to her, because he was afraid of how she would react. Every night she kissed him, but always in the same detached manner of her first night at home from the hospital. Once or twice he tried to kiss her mouth, but she turned her head aside so that the kiss fell on her face. She did, however, develop the habit of clinging to him, and at night would fall asleep lying half across him, with her arms around his neck and waist. This physical closeness made James more aware of the huge emotional distance which there was between them, and he wondered if this distance, this silence and formality, would continue for the rest of their lives. Was this to be his punishment?

As the year progressed, there developed a shift in balance between the couple, which was discernible even to Gerald as he took his lunch in the farmhouse. Jane did begin to recover, but her recovery was matched by the steady decline of her husband, as though he were taking on all her tension and unhappiness. They were themselves conscious of this, but observed it as though it were something happening outside their own selves, as one might have observed the change from winter to spring which was taking place at that time. For just as there are days in winter when early buds are seen; and days in spring when one is surprised by the unexpected severity of a night frost, so too Jane would remark an outburst by James over some trivial matter, and he too would sometimes see in Jane a sudden return to the bristling silence of a day's duration, as though she had completely reverted to the early stages of her illness. And as there are days between the two seasons which are too grey and indifferent to be either winter or spring, so too by late March a visitor to the farm would have found it impossible to tell whether it was Jane or James who had recently suffered from severe depression.

It was on a day in early April that Jane gathered daffodils to put in the parlour, and she was dealing with them in the back scullery when James came in. The flowers and foliage were lying on the wooden drainingboard, and he saw that only on one or two had the tight, greenish yellow petals cracked through the brittle parchment in which they were encased: all the rest were intact and still bright green.

'Jane?'

'Yes?'

'I've just been speaking to Gerald. He told me that Ellen had her baby last night. A boy.'

'Oh.' Jane picked up a vase and filled it from the tap, then one by one she began to put flowers into it. Suddenly she stopped and looked at him sideways. 'It has nothing to do with us, has it?' she said languidly.

She resumed working with the flowers, and James did not reply. He turned to walk away, but had barely reached the kitchen when he heard her crying behind him. He at once turned back, they put their arms around each other, and they both cried.

Then she pointed to the vase upon the drainingboard and she said, 'Wasn't I foolish? I gathered these specially in bud, because I thought that it would be nice to see them open out in the warmth of the house, but I was wrong. They look horrible. They don't look like flowers, they just look like things – stupid-looking green things.' And taking them up in her hand, she snapped off the unopened head of each daffodil in turn.

Loneliness was habit, and habit was comforting. The loneliness of her youth had been so frightening that she married only to escape it, but the image or idea of union did not make union itself. Deep down, the idea of breaking from this habit of loneliness into a new habit – the habit of not being alone – had been more frightening still. She had stayed as she was, almost cherishing her loneliness because it had become, through habit, a part of herself. Now, she genuinely wanted to break out, and accepted that this would mean breaking something in herself.

'It's not a question of children,' she said to James that night.

'Don't you want to have children?' he asked.

'That's not what I meant,' she replied. 'It's not a question of having or not having children. If we do I'll be happy, but if not, well, so be it. But it's not the most important thing. You must know that, James. That's where I went so wrong before.'

'What is it then?'

'I don't know. I mean, I know, but I can't find the words for it. It has to do with just you and me.' She picked up his hand and she kissed it, then stroked it against her face. 'I wish that I could become you, James. I wish that I could be you, while still somehow being myself. Do you understand that?'

'I think so.'

'Do you think that it's possible?'

'I don't know.'

Spring became undeniably spring, with tulips, lambs and rain. Jane planted a small vegetable garden and worked hard to weed and tend it. As she worked, James watched her, and he wished that her illness had left her more tangibly wounded, wished that she had some outward weal or scar so that he could touch the sore place and show that he was not frightened or disgusted. But he realized that this would not have worked; for where he meant a request for forgiveness, Jane would have understood only a show of pity.

Jane noticed how her husband habitually watched her, but she did not understand what it meant. Any attempt to interpret it was complicated by her seeing it in a wider context, for a while James watched her, Jane was conscious that they were both being watched by Gerald. It was a strange experience, for she felt, rather than saw, what was happening, yet knew for certain that it was not just a feeling but a fact. While she worked in the garden or stood by the scullery sink she would suddenly realize that he was looking at her, even if he was out of her line of vision at the time. Stranger still was to notice how particularly he watched James, something of which James appeared to be completely unaware. Jane did not speak of this matter to her husband, because the effect, rather than the act itself, was impossible for her to define. When she felt that they were being watched as a couple, she gave it a name – 'jealousy' – although she knew that jealousy was just a word and not the right word.

But in time she realized that because of her knowledge and her wilful silence, she held the biggest degree of power in the situation. By pretending not to know that she was being watched, she was able to control what Gerald saw, and she ensured that he saw very little. When he watched them as a couple, Jane was careful never to show any sign of intimacy or even affection towards James, for she guessed that that was what Gerald wanted to see, although she could not tell why. Failure to see what he was looking for forced him to watch more carefully still, but Jane was more than a match for him. The situation had a curious effect upon her, and reminded her of something in her past, although at first she could not remember what it was. Then it occurred to her that the sensation created was exactly the same mixture of pleasure and distress which she had known before, but the past cause was a reversal of what was happening now, for she remembered how, before she was married, when she and James would kiss in public, she would feel strangers watching them, and the more she disliked this, the more exciting it made the kissing become.

As spring wore into summer she began to wonder if her wilful use of the wrong word 'jealousy' for what she saw in Gerald could not perhaps be rightly applied to her own feelings towards the family at the cottage. Jane and James never spoke to each other about Ellen and Gerald and Peter, the baby, but Jane thought about them frequently. She could not understand the fascination which they held for her. She did not believe that they were a particularly happy family, so why should she envy them? She felt that she and James would be happier if they could cut the couple out of their lives for ever, but she knew that that would not happen, as they could not leave the farm, and Gerald and Ellen had no intention of leaving the cottage.

She came to James one night at dusk, when he was in the farmyard. All the hay had been cut, and he was standing by the gate, looking out over a field of stacked bales. Jane was about to speak, when James unexpectedly said, 'That Gerald's a fool man. You're never to pay heed to anything he says, Jane. He's not half right in the head. He hasn't said anything to you lately, has he?'

'About what?'

James shrugged. 'About anything. I don't know what sort of rubbish he thinks, but I wouldn't listen to anything he tells you.'

'He hardly ever talks to me at all.'

'Good.'

'James?'

'Yes?'

'I have something to tell you.'

'Tell me, then.'

'I'm going to have another baby.'

James did not speak for some moments, and then he said, 'Are you happy about that, Jane?'

'Yes.' She tapped nervously with her fingernails upon the iron bars of the gate. 'Yes, I am happy. But I'm frightened too.'

Her attitude to this, her second pregnancy, was completely different from her attitude to her first. She made no effort to prepare the nursery, and did not sew or knit clothes for the baby, as she had done before. She was even reluctant to buy baby clothes, and it was only after gentle coaxing from James that she made a brief shopping trip to the city.

'Well, that's that done,' she said to him on her return. She did not remove the shop wrapping paper from the large parcel which she carried, but tossed it unopened into a spare wardrobe.

'Did you get what you wanted?' he asked her.

'I got what will do. I bought a made-up layette rather than bother choosing things individually.'

She was glad to have the chore done, but two weeks later, she had had to go back to the city to buy some more baby clothes, for the doctor had told her that she was going to have twins.

As summer ended, she would walk through all the rooms of the empty house, looking into the mirrors and touching the furniture. In the silence she tried to imagine it as the home in which a family – her family – would live, but she always failed to overcome the idea of it as a place bound to the past. She could think only of the people who had lived there and were now dead, rather than of the people who would live there, and who were yet to be born. Because she had not seen her first baby, the idea of her children was still something abstract to her. Remembering how, as a child, she had longed to see someone whom she resembled physically, she realized that this wish would now perhaps become a reality. But the idea did not fill her with pleasure, and instead she felt frightened to think of it.

The apple crop that year was unusually heavy. Jane gathered up the windfalls in buckets, and James plucked the sound apples from the branches, put them in a big laundry basket and carried them to the attic of the house for Jane to put them in store. She spent many hours sitting there in the gloom of the low-ceilinged room, where the air was sweet with the mingled smell of apples and straw. She sorted the sound fruit from the damaged, wiped the greasy green skins with a clean cloth, and then packed them away in straw, ensuring that no two apples touched. The monotony and the silence of the task soothed her, and as she worked, she thought of nothing.

One morning, however, while she was working in the attic, she heard shouting down in the farmyard. The wind blew away the words so that she could not hear what was being said, but, curious, she crossed to the skylight and opened it. Standing on tip-toe on an upturned box, she could see down into the yard, where James and Gerald were arguing. Gerald was clearly angry, while James looked scornful. Suddenly, she saw Gerald grasp James by the collar, but it was James who lifted his fist as if to hit the other man, and as he did there was a look of such quick violence on his face that Jane turned away. She remembered the day shortly before the wedding of Gerald and Ellen when James had shot the treeful of starlings, and she had watched him then as he trod upon the dying bird. It was the first time she had seen such violence in her husband, and she had looked at it steadily. But now she knew the violence that there was in him, and she could not bring herself to look because it frightened her too much: instinctively she turned away. When she glanced out of the skylight again a few moments later, both the men had gone, and the yard was deserted.

At lunchtime, only James came to the house.

'How are you getting on with the apples?' he asked as soon as he entered.

'All right.'

'Will you be ready for them if I bring in more this afternoon?'

'Yes, I suppose so.'

He washed his hands at the scullery sink, dried them and went up to the kitchen table. Jane waited.

'Oh, by the way,' he said, 'you needn't put out any food for

Gerald today. He's gone home to the cottage for his lunch.'

She did not ask him why: she did not want to hear the blatant lie which he would unblinkingly tell her, for she did not want to see that dishonesty any more than she had wanted to see his violence. But the incident had left her angry and frightened.

After James had eaten his lunch, she removed his plate saying, 'I've changed my mind. You needn't bother bringing me any more apples today. I'm not going to do the apples this afternoon.'

'Why not?'

'I don't want to.'

'Don't you feel well, Jane?'

'I'm all right,' she replied impatiently.

After James had gone back out to the yard, Jane cleared away all the lunch things and tidied the kitchen. Then she left the house and went for a walk alone through the fields, as she had frequently done at the start of that year, while she was recovering from her illness.

It was a cold afternoon, and the grey sky promised rain. Jane pulled her coat more tightly around herself, and plodded on steadily until she reached the lough, having first carefully skirted the cottage. She stood looking over the wide expanse of dull, chill water, and she thought of the winter that soon would come, dreading it as she always dreaded the coming of winter. She could not believe that before the following spring she would be a mother. Putting her hand against her body, she tried to imagine the babies floating inside her, tried to think of life rather than death. Then she realized that her past habitual loneliness had been broken. *'I wish that I could be you, while still somehow being myself.'* Well, that would never be possible with James. She knew that now, had known it for some time, and the incident of that morning was the final proof.

She turned to walk back towards the house, and as she did, she glimpsed Gerald pushing his way through the spindly trees which grew along the shore. He was at some distance from her and was not walking towards her, so she stayed where she was and remained very still, in the hope that he would not see her.

Gerald walked down to the edge of the water. He stopped, took off his jacket and hung it upon a little tree. Then he stepped into the water. The water's coldness was evidently a shock to him at first, but he stepped forwards and steadily began to walk. The bed of the lough shelved gently: he had walked a considerable distance without having reached any significant depth of water.

And then he took one step more and vanished.

Jane, watching from the shore, was amazed by his sudden and complete disappearance. He had not stumbled, nor had he thrown himself into the water, but had taken a single step forwards and gone straight down. She stood there looking at the empty scene before her. *You didn't imagine this,* she told herself. *It really happened. This is real.*

She turned and walked back across the fields, and she thought, *You know what this is, but do you know what it means? You don't know what it means. You can't begin to know what it means.*

As she passed through the farmyard, James spoke to her but she did not answer. She walked silently into the house, went straight upstairs and she lay down on the bed. When James came up to see her still she would not speak, but lay looking at the ceiling and she did not utter a single word.

Ellen missed Gerald by mid-afternoon, and she found his jacket hanging on the tree. When the news was brought to the farm, Jane was still upstairs in bed. She heard James open the front door, heard voices and although she could not hear the words she knew what was being said. She heard James close the front door, pause, then he walked heavily up the stairs and came into the room. She knew what he was going to tell her. He sat down on the bed beside her.

'Jane,' he said very quietly, 'Gerald drowned himself in the lough this afternoon.'

And even as she screamed, she wondered why she was screaming; even as she pulled away from James crying 'No! No! It can't be true,' she could not understand why she should behave like this. Until that moment she had thought that if she had so desired, she could have given the news to James as quietly as he had given the news to her. Now she realized that she had seen but she had not believed, and that James's words alone had made the deed real for her.

'I have to go and help to look for him,' he said. 'I'll be back as soon as I can. Look after yourself until I get back.'

Jane spent the late afternoon sitting by an upstairs window, from which she watched the flotilla of little boats out dragging for the body. They worked all evening until the light failed, by which time they had found nothing. The search was abandoned for the night, to be resumed the following day at first light.

'I suppose it could all be a cod,' James said when he came back to the farm. 'He could just have hung his jacket on a tree to let on. He could have gone off and be lying drunk in a ditch somewhere.'

'I don't think so,' Jane said very quietly.

'What makes you so sure?'

'If he did do it,' she said, as though thinking aloud, 'I wonder what the reason was?'

James did not reply.

The more Jane thought about the incident, the more distressing it became to her. She did not go to bed that night, but sat up in the kitchen, wrapped in a blanket and drinking tea. She thought of his dead body drifting insensible down in the dark water with the weeds, the fish and the eels. It was not the power of the water that shocked her, but Gerald's surrender to it, and even Jane wondered at the depth of self-hate that there must have been in his heart. It had not been his fate, but his will and his choice. Again and again she thought of how easily it had been accomplished, by an act simple and mysterious as a sacrament, but an act of such destruction.

James slept for part of the night, but when he awoke in the early hours of the morning to find that Jane was not by his side he came downstairs. They sat together in the kitchen drinking tea and talking inconsequentially while they waited for dawn to break. When at last they heard the first bird of the day sing they fell silent, and they listened while the clamour of bird-song increased. Darkness faded from the sky.

James had arranged to take part in the search with a man he knew who owned a small boat. He put on his coat and prepared to leave the house, but when he went to open the back door and go out, he suddenly heard her voice say loud and steady behind him:

'I don't care that he's dead. We're not. We're alive.'

He turned around and saw Jane curled up in the old battered armchair, cradling a warm empty teacup in her hands. She was looking away from him as though she had not spoken a word, then she glanced casually in his direction.

'You'd best be off, James.'

She spent all that day again sitting by the upstairs window, watching the boats. In the late afternoon James came home. 'We found him,' he said. Jane nodded.

She asked no questions, and he did not tell her that the body had been found from the boat in which he, James had been sitting, nor did he tell her that they had stopped using nets when they guessed what had happened to him. He had been pulled, by means of a large iron boat-hook, from the sand-pumping pit into which he had stepped. His clenched fists were full of gravel and sand.

Jane did not go to the wake or to the funeral: her pregnancy served as an excuse for her absence. When James came home from the funeral, she was up in the attic putting the last of the apples in store.

'Is he buried, then?'

'Yes.'

'Where did they put him?' She picked up an apple and wiped it slowly. 'In Ellen's family grave?'

'No,' James replied. 'He's at the foot of the hill.'

Jane's hand stayed for only a second. 'Oh,' she said. 'I see.'

She nestled the apple down in straw.

Four months later, Jane gave birth to twin girls, Catherine and Sarah.

Jane and James never spoke of Gerald again.

CHAPTER TEN

'Catherine,' Sarah says.

'Yes?'

'Did you know that we have a brother?'

It is late on a Friday night in March, and the sisters are standing in the kitchen. Their father has long since gone to bed. Weakly Catherine repeats her sister's words. 'We have a brother.'

'Well, we had a brother,' Sarah amends her initial statement. 'Sit down here, Catherine. I'm sorry, I should have broken it to you more gently. Don't upset yourself now, but look here and I'll explain.'

She takes from her pocket two yellowed and creased pieces of paper, and she spreads them out on the table. 'I found an old handbag belonging to Mama the other day. It was away at the back of the attic, and this is what was inside it.' One of the pieces of paper is a birth certificate, one a death certificate.

'Poor, poor Mama. It must have been so sad for her. It happened two years before we were born. Her first baby. Isn't it terrible that we never knew? Don't cry so, Catherine, try not to upset yourself. I wouldn't have told you if I had known that it would upset you so much.' But Catherine is weeping uncontrollably, and Sarah herself is beginning to cry.

'All those years, and she had this secret.'

'Dada too,' sniffs Catherine.

'Yes,' says Sarah, 'Dada too.'

For a moment they do not speak, then Catherine says, 'I think Mama was very brave.'

'Do you? Why?'

'Because of her life. Because she never gave in, she always kept on trying. I loved her for being brave more than I loved her for anything else.'

'I loved her too,' says Sarah, 'but she frightened me. Didn't she frighten you?'

'Yes,' says Catherine. 'A little.' Sarah does not speak and then Catherine says, 'No, that's not true. She frightened me a great deal.'

'Do you remember the day that I told her I didn't believe what she had told us about her childhood? No? Well, I did. I said, "Mama, it's all lies and I don't believe a word of it. You're making it all up so that we'll feel sorry for you."'

'Did you really think that, Sarah? Did you really think that she was lying?'

'In one way, yes, I did. I think most children feel that way about their parents' past lives. You have to take it all on trust, for there's no way that you can ever prove otherwise, and now and then everyone must suspect that they're being lied to. But with Mama it was something more. It wasn't so much that I didn't believe what she told us, it was more that I didn't want to believe. I didn't want to believe that someone I loved had had to suffer so much; and I didn't want to believe that what she said was true because if it was, then it made her even more frightening in herself than she already was. I once read about the daughter of a famous soldier, who said that she was very proud of her father, but I doubted it. I wondered if she felt about him as I felt about Mama. I wondered if she also tried not to believe the truth of all that her father had seen and done and suffered, because I couldn't understand how anyone could live knowing such things about someone whom they loved. So I said it to her plainly, "Mama, I don't believe you."'

'And what did Mama say?'

'She was angry,' says Sarah, smiling a little. 'She was angrier than I ever saw her at any other time in my whole life. Do you know what she did, Catherine? She took hold of my hand and she said that if I didn't apologize and take back what I had said, that she would break my little finger.'

'And did you apologize?' asks Catherine.

'Of course I did. I didn't want to get my little finger broken.'

Catherine looks up in surprise from the two certificates. 'You don't honestly think that she would have done it, do you?'

'She could have. If what she said was true, she was certainly capable of it. And it *was* true. I always knew that, and I always believed it. I just didn't want to believe it.'

They fall silent, as though embarrassed by the honesty with which they speak. They rarely talk about their mother now. As they sit there in the empty kitchen, they can hear the birds crying out in the night, and that also makes Sarah think of her mother, and of her mother's death.

A frosty night has the same effect, for she remembers how she looked up at the starry sky as they followed her into the hospital. Four hours later they walked out again, leaving her dead there; and again Sarah had looked up at the sky where the quiet stars still were shining. Now she saw them differently, but she could not and cannot define the difference: she knows that four hours and the death of one woman does not cause the stars to move in the sky. Later she realized that some of the stars themselves were dead, had died long before her mother's death or even her birth, but their light still shone from a point in space so far distant that it could be measured only in terms of time. And so the dead empty stars still shone, and would shine, even after Sarah's own death. She thinks of how, on that morning, they had driven back to the empty farm, and had walked from room to room. On coming to the kitchen, she heard the farm cat crying in the yard, and because it seemed to be the only creature for whom she could now do anything, she went out and gave it a saucer of milk. Even as she thinks of it she can feel the cat's fur warm against her skin, can feel its head nudge her hand as she pours out the milk, and then the mews change to a contented lapping sound. Sarah looks up. Away in the east the dawn light bleeds up from the horizon into the clouds and the sky. She can see the dark rows of trees and hedges begin to take shape and blacken against the light, as though they are being fleshed out of the darkness itself. And above and beyond everything she hears the cry of invisible birds, caught out there between morning and night. The noise is wild, living, continuous, as though the whole earth is being wrung in re-creation. Never before has she been particularly conscious of the bird-song; has taken it for granted all her life.

Now, two years after the death, she sits in the kitchen and she says to her sister, 'Do you know, I never really noticed the noise of the birds until Mama died. Now I notice it all the time.'

Catherine replies, 'Mama once told me that on the first day she came to this house, before she was married, the sound of the birds was the very first thing that she noticed. Isn't that strange?'

Catherine does not add that until her mother died she had never known what it was to be lonely. Since then, she has known little else.

Again they fall silent, and they are both thinking the same thought: 'Tell her now.' The intimacy and the honesty of the night is unexpected and unusual, and both sisters feel that if ever they can confide in each other, it must be now. Still they do not speak, but they can sense a curious tension, for as they strain for the courage to tell they each become conscious that the other is not sensing this and opening herself to listen, but that she also seems to be on the point of confiding something. And each suddenly feels that the other knows her secret; that she will speak and her sister will reply, 'I know.' The silence strains for a moment longer, then Sarah abruptly begins to fold up the two pieces of paper which are lying on the table. At precisely that moment Catherine rises to her feet, saying, 'I must go on up to bed now. I'm very tired.'

'Yes, you must be. Off you go. Goodnight.'

They both look at each other for a fraction of a second, and they both know that they have failed. They know too that such an opportunity will probably not come again.

'Good night, Sarah. Sleep well.'

'Do you know that you have two great big dark rings under your eyes? Didn't you sleep well last night?'

'No,' replies Sarah.

'You're worried about something,' says Peter, putting his hand up to touch her tired face. 'Tell me what it is.'

And when Sarah hears this she wants to weep, for she remembers that Peter asked her exactly the same question at the start of the year. Soon it will be Easter. All those intervening months now seem to be a failure and a waste, a stupid attempt to pretend that time is not passing. Against the flow of the weeks she has struggled to keep life – all their lives – in stasis. And what frightens her now is to see how nearly she believed that she had succeeded in this. It had been a genuine shock to see in Catherine's face an inkling of knowledge. Now she knows that she had believed and not believed in what she knew about her sister, believed it in her heart, but thought that her silence could hold off reality for ever. Her belief in her sister's fate had been like the belief in resurrection which she had thoughtlessly held from childhood until the day when she looked at her mother's corpse, for she knew then that she could never believe that the dead will rise from the grave. For a moment she wonders if she could be mistaken: could Catherine know something else? But no, she thinks, that is only a cowardly wish and not a realistic hope. Her failure to broach the matter the previous evening fills her with disgust.

And Peter. What of Peter? She has forced him into the same situation; she has made progress of any kind impossible. In January he had wanted to know why she was worried and she did not reply. Now, four months later, when he asks her the same question, still she cannot or will not answer him. If I do not make things change, she thinks, they will change in any case. I cannot control my life or other people's lives by doing nothing. I will tell him now.

She takes his hand in her hands and she steels herself to speak. 'Peter, I . . .' She breaks off and falls silent. Lifting up his hand, she looks at it, then rubs it against her face. Closing her eyes she holds his hand in hers as a child might hold on to a parent, and she strokes the base of his thumb. Then she opens her eyes and she looks at his hand again, turning it curiously this way and that, scrutinizing the length of the fingers and the shape of the nails. Peter is puzzled and embarrassed.

'It's one of a pair, you know,' he says at last, holding up his other hand. Sarah smiles. 'What do you find so interesting in them?'

'Nothing,' she says, now frowning slightly. 'I don't know. I'm sorry, Peter. That must have seemed very odd.' She strokes the back of his hand once more against her face, and then releases him. Glancing up at the clock on the wall she says, 'I must be going now.'

But Peter stops her at the door. 'You were going to say something to me, Sarah. What was it?'

Sarah turns. 'Yes, I was going to say something, Peter. I think that all this has dragged on for far too long, going nowhere. I think that next week, we ought to go to bed together.'

As Sarah is walking home through the fields that afternoon, she finds a bird's nest, blown to her very feet by a fresh spring wind. She stops, stoops and picks it up; cradles it in her hands and admires the beauty of it. The nest is made of interwoven twigs and fine green moss; inside it is smoothly rounded. She will bring it home and show it to Dada: he will be able to tell her what type of bird built it. Suddenly, here in the cold field, she remembers a visit made to the Natural History museum shortly after the death of her mother. She remembers the building's oppressive warmth and the eerie stillness of the stuffed animals, but remembers above all the shock she felt when she saw a bird's nest in a glass case. It was strange that this, the most inanimate object in the museum should be to her the most poignant, but she felt tremendous sadness to look at the dusty, antique nest, and its three blown eggs. Beside the nest was a scrap of yellowed paper, bearing in spiky black writing a date from the end of the last century, a woman's name, and the name of an old demesne familiar to Sarah. Vividly she sees the demesne on a summer evening. The woman is walking. She is wearing a long dress and her hair is pinned up in heavy coils. At a particular tree she stops, and, parting the branches, she reaches up behind soft young leaves to lift down an empty nest. For some moments she stands looking at the nest as it lies there cupped in her hands, and then she decides that she will keep it.

As the sun declines the woman walks home through the innocent wood, while the hem of her long dress trails through the damp grass, and birds sing.

Now the woman and the singing, building birds are all dead, and only the nest remains, holding time like a chalice, holding that summer day, precisely dated on the piece of faded paper, and holding all the lost years that followed until the moment when Sarah stood bereaved before a glass case in a hot, dry museum, envying the woman who found the nest. Two years later, as she stands in the cold field, she knows that were she to put this nest, which she now holds in her livid hands, into a glass box and preserve it for one hundred years, at the end of that time some yet-to-be-born fool would look at the nest and envy Sarah; finding it impossible to take seriously Sarah's suffering, for no other reason than Sarah's distance from her in time.

Why did the woman in the long dress walk alone through the demesne? Did she seek out the nest or did she find it by hazard? Did she hold it in her hands and see in it her own mortality? Even as she touched it, did she not know that the nest would long outlast her, and that another woman would look on it when she had become forgotten dust with the bird that built it?

The woman is standing in her bedroom. The thick coils of hair have been unpinned and brushed out, and show long and dark against her white nightdress. She picks up the nest once more and looks at it, then places it on the window-sill and gets into bed, between stiff white sheets, which smell of lavender. She dims the lamp until the room is filled with perfect darkness. Lying alone in bed, the woman begins to cry quietly.

Sarah starts to walk again, and as she plods along, another meaning for the nest comes to her, a bawdy meaning, and it suddenly seems curiously apt that the nest should have been blown to her feet as she walked from the cottage today.

When she reaches the farm, Catherine is not in the scullery, nor in the kitchen, nor in the parlour. Sarah looks in all the rooms of the house, and at last she finds her sister lying in bed.

'What are you doing here, Catherine?'

'I came up to lie down for a while. I felt tired.'

'Just tired? Sarah asks.

Catherine looks at her sideways. 'I had a slight pain here, but it's gone now. I just need to have a little rest. In any case,' Catherine says in almost apologetic tones, 'I'm going to see the doctor again on Tuesday. What's that you're holding in your hands, Sarah?'

They both know that she is trying to change the subject. Sarah replies shortly, 'A bird's nest.'

'Oh, let me see it.'

Catherine props herself up on her elbow, and takes the nest into her hands. As she examines it, Sarah looks down on the crown of her sister's bowed head, and she wonders just how much Catherine knows, just how much she has guessed.

'Where did you find this?'

'In the field. Lying on the ground. It must have blown out of the hedge.'

To ask would be to tell. Sarah knows how shrewd Catherine can be, knows that her sister can see and understand things where others would remain ignorant. It seems impossible that she does not know: but if she does, could she really lie here so calmly looking at the nest? Only an hour ago Sarah had been convinced that Catherine knew the truth, but now she is not so sure. Perhaps she scarcely suspects what is wrong.

'It's very pretty.' Catherine lifts her head, and as she hands the nest back to her sister, Sarah knows that she has understood nothing from it.

'Rest a while longer,' she says. 'I'll see to Dada's tea.'

Quietly, she leaves the room.

CHAPTER ELEVEN

On the afternoon of her daughters' sixteenth birthday, Jane watched James as he worked in the farmyard. She did not watch him directly, but by means of a large mirror which hung on the kitchen wall, facing the window. James's glance was suddenly reflected straight into her eyes without any flicker of recognition crossing his face, and only then did she realize what she was doing. When James looked through the window he could see only her back: he did not know that he was being watched. Once, Jane would have been proud of such a trick, but now she felt ashamed to have done it, even inadvertently, and she moved away from the mirror.

Only the previous evening she had surprised Sarah before it, for on coming into the room she had found her daughter staring transfixed at her own reflection. Jane had said nothing in the face of Sarah's confusion, but now she wondered what her daughter was looking for; wondered if Sarah needed to stare so intently to see what she, Jane, had glimpsed so vividly in a cheval glass when she herself was little older than Sarah. *My children are not children any more*, she thought: *or rather, they are shaking off childhood in the odd ways of adolescence.* While Sarah stared at herself in mirrors, Catherine obsessively kept a huge diary, and Jane frowned as she thought of the latter. She often wondered about Catherine: there was in her a piousness, a priggishness almost, which her mother disliked, and which seemed to be at odds with other aspects of her personality. For Jane, what was so frustrating about her daughters was that she felt she ought to understand them, and quite often she almost did, but could never get beyond that 'almost'. Some little points of knowledge or sympathy always shimmered just out of Jane's access or understanding, and the older her daughters became the more conscious she was of this. She tried not to let it upset her, or make her resentful: but it did make her feel strange. Strange too was the sensation of seeing fragments of herself and James in their daughters' faces and bodies, in their habits and mannerisms, and in the inflexions of their voices. Perhaps it frustrated her not to be able to fully understand her daughters, because it felt like a failure to understand herself. She realized now that when she looked into the face of either Catherine or Sarah, she felt as though she were looking into a mirror, the reflection of which was not quite true. The essence of herself was hidden in her daughters, and she could never quite find it. She wished that today she could say to Catherine and Sarah, 'Have I been a good mother to you?' but then felt sad, because she realised the futility of such a question.

Crossing to the window, she looked out into the farmyard where James was working. He was removing the downspout from the wall of the shed, and this puzzled her, for he had not mentioned that it needed to be mended, nor had she noticed anything wrong with it.

Having worked loose the last screws, James wrenched the downspout free from its brackets and shook it hard. A little brown sparrow tumbled out stunned upon the ground. It lay there for a moment, made a few abortive hops across the yard, lay again, and then made a short, uncertain flight to a nearby wall, where it was out of reach of the farm cat, and could sit to recover itself fully before flying away. Jane saw James watch the bird's shaky progress, then he turned back to the downspout, and began to fix it to the wall again.

Suddenly she said aloud to James, 'It wasn't my fault.' But she had forgotten the pane of glass which separated them, and James worked on oblivious. It was two months to the day since her pains had begun, pains which she kept secret from everyone, for her childhood fear of hospitals remained, and this was sufficient to help her hide her illness from all around her. Gripping the edge of the window-sill, she slowly counted to twenty. The pain subsided, but she knew in her heart that she could not hold it off for ever simply by secrecy and silence.

James had finished his work at the downspout, and was

coming towards the farm. Turning away from the window, Jane prepared to smile and greet him.

Five nights after their sixteenth birthday, Catherine and Sarah awoke just after midnight to the sound of their father's voice.

'That's blood, Jane,' he was saying, 'nothing but pure, pure blood. Christ, Jane, don't die on me . . . don't die, please don't die.'

The sisters arose from their beds and hurried to their parents' bedroom. The door was open and the light was on. Jane lay on the floor where she had evidently fallen, and James knelt beside her, half cradling her in his arms. The bottom half of Jane's nightdress and an alarmingly large part of the carpet on which she lay was darkly stained with blood. Her face was very pale and she was shivering, but she was fully conscious. When her daughters came into the room and stood staring in horror, she looked at them askance, as though they had surprised their parents in something intimate, and should have had the decency to go away again at once.

'Go one of you downstairs and phone for an ambulance,' said James.

'No,' said Jane quickly.

'Do as I say!' James shouted. Sarah ran from the room.

'I want a drink of water,' Jane said, and Catherine was about to go and fetch one for her when James said, 'No. When you get to the hospital, they might want to operate on you, and you're not allowed to drink before an operation.'

'I'm not going to the hospital,' Jane said stubbornly. She was still shivering. 'I want a drink.'

'For Christ's sake have sense, Jane,' James cried. 'You can't lie here on the carpet until you bleed to death. Of course you'll have to go to the hospital.'

Jane began to cry querulously.

'I don't want them to operate on me. I don't want to go to hospital. It's not fair, James. I want a drink of water, and I'm cold.'

More gently now, James said to her, 'Jane, you don't know

what it is to me not to be able to give you a drink, but I can't. Your life might depend on it.' Reaching behind him, he pulled two blankets off the bed and wrapped them around Jane. He held her tightly in his arms and told her not to cry.

By the time the ambulance arrived, she was too weak to protest about going to hospital, and the two blankets, like the nightdress and the carpet, were heavily stained with blood. She was taken away by strangers: the family followed behind in the car.

At the hospital, they were made to wait for a long time in the corridor while the doctors worked on Jane. When at last they went into the stiflingly warm little ward, they tried hard not to show the shock which they felt to see the wires, the flickering monitors, and the little plastic bagful of blood which hung above the bed, and which was connected to Jane's arm by a thin tube. She was, despite all this, still conscious.

'I feel a bit better now,' she said. 'I'm not as cold as I was when I was in the house.' Her voice was very weak, and James had to put his ear close to her mouth to hear what she was saying.

'Tell the girls to go out again for a moment,' she said. 'I want to talk to you alone.'

Catherine and Sarah left the little ward. A nurse hovered around the other bed, while James leaned over his wife.

'James,' she whispered, 'I'm going to die.'

'No you're not,' he said desperately. 'I thought you might in the house, but now you're going to be all right. Now you're in the best place.'

'I'm going to die, James, I know it.'

'Perhaps you shouldn't talk, Jane. You're only upsetting yourself. Try to save your energy.'

She closed her eyes and was quiet for a while, until James began to wonder if she had fallen asleep, or even into a coma, when she whispered something more. He did not catch what it was, and he leaned over her more closely.

'I said: what will you do without me?'

'Don't ask me that,' he pleaded. 'You'll be better, Jane, in time.'

'No,' she said. 'You'll be lonely, James. Once it would have worried me. When I was young, I was jealous: you know that.'

There were long pauses between each sentence, and she smiled faintly. 'If I had been dying in the first years after our marriage, my biggest worry would have been that you would marry someone else. That or you'd marry Ellen.'

James smiled uncomfortably, and stroked her hand.

'I could marry her yet,' he said teasingly, but as soon as the words were out, he regretted them. Jane did not seem upset, however, but thoughtful.

'No, you couldn't. A man can't marry his half-sister. Your daddy told me that. In the garden. At the wedding. When was that, James? How long ago?'

He did not answer.

'I'm confused now,' she whispered. 'And I'm tired. I'm so tired, James.'

The nurse came over to the bed, and asked him to leave the ward for a moment.

When James stepped out into the corridor, he was crying. Catherine and Sarah, on seeing his face, understood something different, and when the doctor came out some time later to tell them that Jane had died (and died more suddenly at the end than they had expected would be the case), he was surprised to find that the whole family was already in tears.

CHAPTER TWELVE

Sarah is standing before the kitchen mirror. She has been looking at the reflection of her own face for hours, until it has become strange to her, until it has disintegrated and become meaningless; and until it has become familiar again. Enormous self-hatred is born of this familiarity; it is more than she can bear. Raising her arm she walks towards the mirror, but when she strikes it it does not break. Instead, the mirror yields as though it were made not of glass but of vertical water, and Sarah passes through to the other side. She thinks with relief, *It's over now: I will never again have to look at my own hateful face,* but when she turns around she finds to her horror that the back of the mirror also offers a perfect reflection. In anger and fright she beats upon the mirror, which now behaves as the glass which it is, and shivers into a million bits. The broken shards cut into her hands and her wrists, but still she continues to thrash forwards, until her hands are dripping with blood.

She awakens to the warm, empty silence of her bedroom at night, and her soft, clenched hands are intact and not bleeding. For a moment she is frightened, not because she thinks that she is dreaming still, but because in the confusion of waking she thinks that she is lying still beside Peter. She feels again for a moment the shock of that, for after they had made love what she felt was not a mild sadness, but a devastating loneliness, and despair to find that the complete oblivion which she had wanted had passed her by.

'Are you all right?' Sarah does not reply, and Peter moves to kiss her again, but she turns her head aside and she wishes for the blackness which there is now, in the night, when she is again alone. But turning back quickly she leans her face against him thinking, life, what is it only this? A steady beat in the chest rather than silence, a body that is warm and moving rather than one that is still and cold.

When she arrived at the cottage that afternoon, he had brought her to his bedroom and left her alone there for some moments. She had not been in his room for years, and although she recognized certain of his possessions, the overall effect was of great strangeness. She felt as though she were in a stranger's room. All the objects which she saw there should have given her clues about the identity and personality of the room's owner, but instead confused her. Picking up a book from the table beside the bed she turned aside. It seemed impossible that the person who would read such a book would choose to wear the clothes she saw hanging on the back of a chair. The apparent incompatibility of all these things made her doubt the truth and reality of the person for whom she waited. The created persona did not ring true. She was suspicious and frightened. *But I do know him*, she thought, *I know him better than I know anyone else, apart from Catherine and Dada.* When she called to him then, she tried to be casual, and was surprised by the panic in her own voice which she found she could not control. 'Peter,' she said loudly, 'Peter, come here to me now.'

Was it because she had been so foolish as to imagine all these things that his face looked ridiculously familiar when he came back into the room (a room which at once looked perfectly natural as his home, a room utterly artless in its arrangement)? He did not merely look familiar: he looked too familiar, and now, in the night, as she remembers that moment, Sarah remembers also the moment in the dream from which she has just awoken, when the image of her own face was over familiar to her, and disturbing. *How well do I know him*? she had thought as he came towards her. *In some ways I know him as well as I know myself, and in others, I don't know him at all.* In the dream mirror the thick glass had been bevelled at the edges, and caught the light in colours, which showed as they would show in the water, air and light of a rainbow, but when she moved her head there was a point, a fine, fine line at which the colours vanished, and then she could see only the thick green of the glass. When she made love with Peter, her knowledge of him shimmered on just so fine an edge, between knowing everything and knowing nothing.

When she thinks of it now, already she can think of it with a certain cold distance, for already it is in the past. That distance was already there when she left the cottage to come home. She had thought that she might feel shame, guilt or regret, but instead she felt nothing at all. The feelings of strangeness and loneliness had passed, and she sensed only that she had failed in whatever her obscure purpose had been.

On returning to the farm, Sarah found the kitchen empty. She went to Catherine's room, fearing to find her in bed again, but that room was also deserted. She stood for a few moments looking around her sadly, as she had looked around Peter's room. The same feeling of strangeness and contrivance was there, the same difficulty in believing the reality of the person who lived there. *I know Catherine. She is my sister. I know her.* Her gaze came to rest upon the big thick diary which sat upon the bedside table. A little thought then spawned in her mind. Shocked, she quashed it, and turned away.

But the little thought returned and returns; comes to her now in the night, and it grows into schemes which she turns over shamefully in her mind as she lies here in the blackness. She does not reject these plans, but perfects and attempts to rationalize them, even though she knows that what she is considering is wrong.

The following day is Sunday, when Catherine rarely does any work, but today she does nothing at all, and leaves the preparation of all the meals to Sarah.

'What's wrong with you?' Sarah asks.

'I'm tired,' is all she will reply.

Sarah does not dare to press her further, but now it is of supreme importance that she knows the extent of Catherine's knowledge. On the Sunday night she again lies awake for hours, and the memory of Peter barely enters her mind: instead she is thinking of her sister, and thinking of her plan.

On the Monday morning Catherine does not appear in the

kitchen. Sarah goes to her room, and finds her awake but still in bed.

'Will I call the doctor?'

'No.'

'Well, if you're sick . . .'

'I'm sick, but I'm not so very sick.'

Sarah leaves her, and does the morning chores on the farm. On the kitchen table, Catherine's diary is sitting where Catherine wrote in it the night before, and neglected to put it away. Its usual place by her bedside is due to habit and convenience, not mistrust of her family. Sarah's every second thought is with the book, and her glance is drawn to it again and again.

In the early afternoon, Catherine says to Sarah, 'Perhaps I was wrong. Perhaps you should phone for the doctor.'

'I probably won't be able to get him now. You should have allowed me to call him this morning.'

'He'll come for me,' says Catherine quietly. Sarah knows that she is right, and her sister's confidence frightens her. It is later, when the doctor is with her sister, that she decides what she will do, and her resolution is as firm and as cold as her choice concerning Peter. When the doctor has finished, she politely sees him out, and is uneasy when he tells her that he has given Catherine a shot which will make her sleep until morning. It is as if fate is conspiring with her in what she is planning to do. She waits that night until her father has gone to bed, and then she sits down at the kitchen table, and she draws Catherine's diary towards her. She is fully conscious that what she is doing is irrevocable, and that she is unlikely ever to forget anything which she is about to see. Then she thinks of Peter, shrugs, and opens the book.

Sarah turns at first to the most recent pages, and finds in essence what she had hoped and expected would be there. Catherine knows that she is ill, but is not aware of just how ill, although the doubt and suspicion is clearly there: 'I wonder sometimes just how serious it is, for I cannot believe that something so painful and which has gone on for so long can be insignificant. But how serious is serious?' Her sister's want of full knowledge makes Sarah want to weep, and she is sad to learn that Catherine has suffered much more than she has ever admitted.

So she does not know. But this thought is at once followed by a realization that simply because Catherine's diary is written for herself alone it is not by necessity honest. Perhaps her need to lie and to conceal her knowledge of the truth from herself is even greater than her need to hide it from her sister. Sarah knows then the emptiness of her act. She has broken faith with her sister, and she has learnt nothing.

But health is not her sister's only preoccupation. As Sarah leafs through the diary she is surprised at the frequency with which her own name and Peter's occur. She tries to resist reading in detail, but just as she is about to close the book she sees a paragraph in which their names are mentioned together.

Sarah does not doubt for a moment the truth of what Catherine has written. She knows now what she should have guessed long ago; what her sister guessed and knew from the same too-familiar features which so recently puzzled her. Sarah quickly closes the book and pushes it away from her.

The following morning, Catherine wakes early. She lies in bed thinking of the doctor's visit; and she remembers falling into a deep sleep soon after his departure. She can hear Sarah moving about in other parts of the house, but she does not come to her sister's room. Catherine waits. Time passes, and still Sarah does not come. Catherine begins to feel afraid. She resolves to wait until her sister enters of her own free will, but at last her nerve breaks. Hearing her sister's step outside her door she calls loudly, 'Sarah? Sarah, come in to me here.'

Sarah quietly enters the room. She does not look up. She has been crying, and she does not speak. Catherine had planned to ask her straight out: 'What did the doctor say?' but she cannot manage it; nor can she manage the fatuous requests which she had held in reserve: 'Will you open the window for me, will you bring me a drink?' She says nothing at all, but she turns her face away, and instinctively puts her hands over her eyes.

The door of the bedroom clicks closed as Sarah goes out.

EPILOGUE

'Did you rise before the dawn to see the sun dance?'

It is Easter Sunday morning. Catherine is holding a cup of tea, and on the bedside table there is a chocolate egg wrapped in brightly coloured tinfoil. Both of these things have just been given to her by her sister, who smiles now and says, 'Of course I didn't. I say every year that I will, but you know that I never do.'

'I should have risen myself,' says Catherine, 'this year above all.' Sarah does not reply, and Catherine sips the hot, sweet tea. Suddenly, Sarah leaves the room, and Catherine lies back upon the pillows, utterly dispirited. But she is wrong in what she has understood by this, because Sarah returns quickly, carrying the delft bowl in which five pink tulips have blossomed to perfection. She clears a space on the bedside table, and sets the bowl down. For a moment, the sisters admire the flowers in silence.

'The nice thing is,' Catherine says at last, 'that when the flowers fade, you can plant the bulbs out in the garden, and then they'll come up again year after year, like the daffodils on the big demesne.'

'Yes.'

When Sarah glances from the stiff formal tulips to her sister's face, she sees there suddenly her own mortality. The previous night she had gone to church in the hope of finding some comfort, but in the ceremonial fire, the water and the light, she had found instead that there were things beyond comfort. Now she knows that such things must be recognized, and that to seek to be comforted for them is worse than cowardly, it is merely banal. She also knows to hold her imagination well back from any notion of redemption, resurrection, or how the look of the room will affect her when her sister is gone.

'Sarah?'

'Yes?'

'Open the window for me, please.'

The spring air is cool, and the sisters can hear more clearly now the noise of the birds.

'Will you leave me now for a while? I want to sleep again.'

'Yes.'

Sarah lifts the empty teacup, and Catherine says, 'Thank you again for the chocolate egg.'

As she speaks, Sarah is crossing the room. She stops by the door, turns and looks back at the thin face upon the pillow. The sisters both smile. Then Sarah shrugs, and she says lightly, 'Happy Easter, Catherine.'

'Happy Easter.'

WEXFORD
COUNTY
LIBRARY